Catch a Falling Star

KING OF PENTACLES

Allyson James

ELLORA'S CAVE
ROMANTICA PUBLISHING

An Ellora's Cave Romantica Publication

www.ellorascave.com

Catch a Falling Star

ISBN 9781419958632
ALL RIGHTS RESERVED.
Catch a Falling Star Copyright © 2008 Allyson James
Edited by Mary Altman & Kelli Kwiatkowski.
Cover art by Syneca.

This book printed in the U.S.A. by Jasmine-Jade Enterprises, LLC.

Electronic book Publication July 2008
Trade paperback Publication February 2009

CATCH A FALLING STAR

ॐ

King of Pentacles

The King of Pentacles appears as a wealthy king seated on a throne—or occasionally a horse or chariot—wearing sumptuous robes. A castle rises in the background, and his abundant riches surround him.

Connected to the element of Earth, the King of Pentacles is a true leader—his characteristics are steadfastness and reliability and skill at almost anything. His abilities bring wealth, but in a comfortable, not extravagant, way. He is wise and generous, sharing his abundance with others and helping those in need. Anyone seeking the King of Pentacles would be protected and sheltered and come away stronger.

Chapter One
Pamaar

ဆာ

A star fell from the blackness of space, streaking through the night in a cacophony of red, blue and yellow.

When the star falls, the queen will come and the world will be reborn.

Thane, naked at the window, gripped the sill with a sinewy hand. "Deon."

Behind him on the bed, a dark bulk of a man made a snorting noise and drifted deeper into sleep.

"Deon."

Another loud snort then Deon sat straight up, his long black braids hanging across a hard face, forehead tattooed with a single pentacle. He reached for the sword he kept leaning next to the bed, instantly alert.

"What? What's wrong?"

"A falling star."

"What?"

"Focus, my friend," Thane said impatiently. "A falling star."

Deon rumbled like an annoyed bear. "What about it?"

"The seer. You remember? All of two days ago?"

The three interlaced pentacles on Thane's forehead seemed to burn. He'd called the seer in an attempt to reassure his people that the land was not dying, that he at thirty years old had not yet lost his grip on the kingdom.

The ceremony had backfired when the seer confirmed that Thane's powers had dropped a long way from when he'd first become king at twenty. His power to heal had diminished, and with it, the fertility of the land.

His rivals in the falcon-sword clan had brightened. When the king could no longer function as king, he should allow himself to be slain in single combat in order for a new and stronger king to rise. In this case, the leader of the falcon-sword clan, Felin, was next in line to inherit the kingship of Pamaar.

Thane's men of the lion-star clan had muttered among themselves, knowing their power was diminishing slowly but surely. Then the seer had proclaimed, *When the star falls, the queen will come and the world will be reborn.*

And a star had just fallen.

Did it mean this woman would help Thane regain his powers? Or that he would die and Felin would assume rule of Pamaar?

Deon rubbed his face, starlight gleaming on the lion tattoo that encircled his right arm. "I remember. Anyway, the star watchers say falling stars are burning pieces of rock caught in the atmosphere. Whatever that means. My mother always said it was the death of a fairy, but you know she was crazy. She thought trees talked to her."

Thane couldn't help a smile. "Do you believe in anything, my friend?"

"Just my sword."

"Which one?"

Deon snorted with laughter. "You're funny for a man awake in the middle of the night. A man who just pulled me out of a dream about three women and who will likely be skewered for it."

Deon was the only person in the kingdom who could joke in this fashion with the king. Deon of the night-dark eyes was Thane's personal guard and his loyalty was unquestioned. They'd been friends since childhood and lovers since adulthood, even though Thane had been royal and Deon the son of a weapon maker.

They shared everything now—quarters in the palace, meals, courtesans. Thoughts, dreams and troubles.

"One thing is certain," Thane continued. "Felin will try to find that falling star and what it means. Get a team together and go investigate. I want to know where it came down, if it did come down."

Deon regarded him in surprise. "You know seers, Thane. They say something cryptic to stir up everyone and pretend they know what they're talking about. He probably meant something obscure would happen that no one would understand but him."

"Felin will go."

"Good. Let him and his falcon-boys run around in the middle of the night."

Thane rested his bare backside on the windowsill and folded his arms over his chest. "Humor me."

Deon regarded him a moment then heaved a sigh and kicked the last of the covers from his body. "Oh all-fucking-right."

"Even if it means nothing," Thane said as he watched Deon pull leather leggings and a tunic over his body, "I have to act as though I am doing something about it."

Deon paused as he laced up his shirt. "I'll not let Felin kill you. I'll defend you to my last breath. I made that pledge, and I meant it."

"Very poetic. But I don't want to have to see you do it."

Deon grinned. "You won't. I'll gut that bastard if he comes near you." He strapped his sheathed sword around his waist then tucked knives on various parts of his person. "I'll go find your falling star for you."

"Thank you."

Deon paused to stroke Thane's cock with the palm of his hand and slant a brief kiss across his mouth. "Don't wait up."

He strode out the door, calling for his team to get their asses in gear and follow him.

* * * * *

Please, goddess, let me land on something soft.

The controls on Lea's scout ship had gone completely. She hung on to the steering shaft of the one-man craft and cursed her mechanic, her team leader, her onboard computer, the asshole who'd shot her down and the entire Four-One-Six Quad Empire, who were gearing up to steal huge chunks of her home world's territory.

Her world, officially called *sector eighteen, coordinates zero zero six seven one* and fondly called The Rock, would never be able to attack the empire. They could only defend, hence the scouting missions to find out where and when the empire's harvester ships might strike.

Lea had come far too close to a harvester — had to in order to skim data from their communications stream — then one of her shields had failed and she'd been seen.

So now her scout ship plummeted straight for this unknown planet that wasn't on any of her charts. It showed up on none of the readouts scrolling haphazardly past her eyes — it was simply a blob of blue and green coming up way too fast.

Her only satisfaction was that she'd been able to cripple one of the harvester's outriders and they hadn't fired a finishing shot to kill her. Not that they needed to. Her controls had fried and she'd veered straight into the gravity well of this planet.

Her ship screamed into the atmosphere, the pressure outside the titanium shell increasing every second. The vessel rocked and banged as though it careened through a canyon and protective webbing automatically shot from their casings to wrap her body.

Would it do any good? She'd soon find out.

The impact seemed to happen in slow motion—crumpling metal, blue-white fire, shards of transparent titanium raining over her, the terrible screech of ship against rock. The tiny ship rolled over and over in dizzying spins and then mercifully, Lea blacked out.

When she swam back to consciousness her first thought was, *I'm still alive.*

Her second was, *Oh shit, am I in pain.*

The third was, *Someone is poking me. With a stick.*

She opened her eyes groggily. The safety webbing twined around her body had saved her life, though her insides felt like someone had shaken everything out and put them back in the wrong way. Her helmet was already off—when had that happened?—and she breathed fresh, clear air of unpolluted outdoors.

The end of something long tentatively tapped her side. Gray light of early morning showed her a pole made of wood, shined and polished to rich darkness and carved with strange, intricate symbols.

The pole was held by a brute of a man with a falcon tattoo on one bicep and a sword tattoo on the other. His face was covered with whorls of blue over which dark brown eyes peered at her in curiosity, not fear.

He poked her gently again as though wondering if she were alive and, if so, what would she do?

Why should he be afraid? she thought. *I'm laying half-conscious in a wreck and he has the long stick.*

"Is that a pole in your hand or are you just happy to see me?" she grated.

The man said something over his shoulder. His voice was clear, but the words were nonsense to her.

A second man came to look over his shoulder. He was even bigger than the first, and his studded leather shirt bared arms that would make a prize-winning bodybuilder envious. He had the falcon emblem tattooed on his face, one on either cheek, and his arms bore sword tattoos, lots of them. An earring, a swirl of silver, dangled from his right lobe.

This man dropped to one knee and touched the webbing. He said something she didn't understand, his voice rising in a questioning tone. At least she thought it was a questioning tone—he might be saying bad things about her mother and she'd never know.

Come to think of it, why *didn't* she know his language? As a scout, she'd trained in all the dialects of the empire. Her databanks should have at least given her a sample of this language, but it sounded like pure gibberish.

"I don't know," she said. "I don't understand you—hey!"

He grasped the top of her flight suit and ripped it open to her navel. The body-hugging suit, made to keep out radiation and other nasty things encountered in space, was worn over bare skin. The falcon-man looked at her naked torso and smiled, not a nice smile. He said something to pole-man behind him, and pole-man laughed.

"Rape is against intergalactic law in all ways, shapes and forms," she reminded him in a hard voice.

The man's response sounded neutral, neither gloating nor apologetic. She had the feeling that he didn't know about intergalactic law and probably didn't care.

Where the hell am I?

Falcon-man touched the webbing again, trying to figure out how to loosen it. She didn't help him. The webbing would stay in place until it sensed that she was not likely to be buffeted by the ship any longer. Or until she was dead.

There were trigger points where a rescuer could remove the webbing and drag her body out. The man didn't seem to know where they were—he tugged at the web and ran his hands over it until he found a trigger point by accident.

The webbing stretched once then receded, disappearing into the slots from whence it came. Or almost. The slots had broken with the ship, so most of the webbing hung limp like a man exhausted after all-night sex.

She expected the two primitive-looking men to express surprise at the mechanism—maybe grunt and point?—but falcon-man only looked satisfied and started to pull her free.

Lea had contingencies for hostiles. As the man reached to lift her out of the ruined pilot's pod, she reached behind her, fished her pistol from its holster and shot him.

The pistol was on its lowest setting and should have given him a mild shock, enough to let her get free. She had no intention of leaving a trail of dead bodies as she fled back home—she wasn't that kind of girl. And you had to be careful who you killed or you might accidentally start an intergalactic war.

But the pistol didn't do what she intended. Falcon-man grunted and fell all right, but he was up again in an instant.

That shouldn't have happened. She stared at the pistol, but the indicator light showed it fully charged and hot. The burst should have left the man moaning quietly for about half an hour.

She flicked the setting one higher and shot again. This burst caught falcon-man in the side and he went down, but he was up and back to her before she could catch her breath, his heavy hand twisting the pistol from her grasp.

She braced herself for him to use the weapon on her, but he only held the pistol in his palm and looked it over. He'd clearly never seen such a weapon before, but he carefully kept the muzzle pointed away from himself while he checked out the lights and buttons. He handed the pistol to pole-man, who also gave it a curious once-over.

Then falcon-man got back down on his knees and searched Lea's immobile body. He pulled out her ident card, her less-than-tasty nutrition bars, her short knife in its

15

aluminum sheath, her emergency anti-radiation dose and the bloodstone she kept on a chain for luck.

Some luck. She was alive, but whether that was lucky or not remained to be seen.

Falcon-man peered at the bloodstone, then another smile creased his mouth as he lifted the chain around his neck. Lea burned with fury but there wasn't much she could do.

Firing the pistol had taken the last of her strength. She could only gasp in pain as the man hauled her out of the cockpit and over his shoulder and carried her away.

* * * * *

Deon caught up with Felin and his men before they had time to leave the valley where the fireball had landed. Deon let his warriors engage Felin's fighters and spurred his fire-drake to follow Felin, who was trying to sneak away with whatever he had strapped across his saddle.

Felin had to choose between fighting and holding onto his burden. Deon flew his drake directly at him and knocked Felin out of the saddle. He tasted satisfaction when the man fell about fifteen feet and landed heavily on his back.

The bundle Felin had been trying to protect remained fixed to the saddle as Felin's drake touched down next to his master. Deon ignored the groaning Felin and landed near the man's drake.

Deon had a knack for animals, everyone in the kingdom said. He made clicking noises to the drake, who calmed and let Deon approach him.

The bundle on the saddle turned out to be a battered female in strange garb. Her garment had been torn open, giving him a glimpse of smooth, bare torso and lovely breasts as he pulled her from the saddle. She managed to stand on her feet—just—but she obviously needed healing and had no strength to fight him.

She had no tattoos of any kind, at least none he could see. Strange. Courtesans sometimes kept their tattoos small and hidden, but she did not have the sultry look of a courtesan. Her eyes were a strange, pale jade green, and she glared at him in un-sultry anger.

Felin moved. The man was still on his back, but something gleamed in his hand and a hot bolt suddenly bit into Deon's side.

He yelped and fell to one knee. "What the fuck?"

Felin grinned evilly. He held a small, cylindrical object the like of which Deon had never seen and began touching blinking jewel-like buttons on it.

The woman staggered forward and kicked the object from Felin's hand. As the thing skittered across the rocky ground, a bolt streaked from it and sliced a boulder clean in half. The two sides of the rock fell apart and smoke drifted lazily into the air.

Both drakes screeched and flapped skyward, flying away hard and fast while Felin and Deon stared at the rock in amazement.

"Shit!" Deon shouted to his drake, "Come back here, you pox-rotted coward!"

The drakes paid no attention. Deon looked back in time to see Felin crawling for the weapon. The woman had collapsed to the ground after the kick and lay motionless.

Deon scrambled for the weapon and reached it a split second before Felin did. He snatched it up and held it the way he'd seen Felin do, round cylinder pointed at Felin. Felin fell back, watching Deon warily.

"What the hell is this thing?" Deon demanded. It had buttons down its handle and colored lights, the red one the brightest.

"Screw yourself," Felin spat.

"You didn't know it could break the boulder any more than I did. The only one of us not surprised was her." He glanced at the woman on the ground.

How badly she was hurt he couldn't tell, and she might be less incapacitated than she let on. Her clothes had fallen open again, revealing lush, round breasts his hands itched to explore.

"Did you try to have her?" Deon asked Felin, then grinned. "Let me guess, she said no."

"You rushed out here to fetch her like a dog for his master," Felin countered. "Woof, woof. Good dog."

"Your insults grow more feeble every time we meet, my friend."

"What's your reward when you return with the bone? I know, you get to sample the royal cock. You enjoy having a king in your mouth? Or better, in your ass?"

"Hmm, not as good as the dog thing."

"Bite me, king's man," Felin snarled.

"Don't you wish."

"He's dying, Deon." Felin's tone turned serious. "He's fading and he's taking the rest of us with him. You'd let the entire world grow weak and unguarded because you like his probing tongue? Put your sword through him before it's too late."

Deon's anger boiled, partly because he knew Felin was right. Thane's strength and his protection of the world were fading. The man he'd loved from boyhood had lost so much power and, strong as Deon was, he couldn't stop it.

There were plenty of legends of fading kings who ended their lives in the Challenge so that the leader of the succeeding clan could strengthen the Wards around the kingdom again. But those sacrificing kings had mostly been very old men. Thane was young—barely a quarter of his life had passed.

Thane knew he didn't have much choice. He'd already told Deon that if he couldn't go out in a blaze of glory in the Challenge, Deon would have to perform the task of ending his life.

Hell of a thing to ask your best friend, Deon had growled.

Thane had turned to him, his eyes darker than midnight. *You're the only one I'd trust to do it fast and sure.*

Deon growled now at Felin, "You *really* want me to waste you, don't you?"

"You know it's true. The Wards are already weak. She came from the sky in a metal object, like from the old legends before the first Warding. She should not have been able to."

Deon hid his worry by scowling. "You talk too much."

"You're not stupid, much as you pretend to be. Join me and his ending will be quick and painless, I promise."

Deon drew his sword and smashed the hilt against Felin's head and, with a grunt, Felin fell back, unconscious.

"Thought he'd never shut up," Deon muttered.

He searched Felin's inert body, pulling out metallic objects as foreign-looking as the weapon. He turned to the woman. "What are these?"

She stared back at him uncomprehendingly. He tried the dialects of other clans but gave up when she clearly didn't understand.

Deon's drake landed behind him, sending up a puff of dirt and grass. The woman tried to scramble away, staring in abject terror as the drake lumbered to Deon and lowered his pointed snout to Deon's shoulder.

"What's the matter?" Deon asked the woman. "He's harmless. A real sweetie."

At that moment, the drake swung his face against Deon's body, sending him staggering sideways. Deon snarled and smacked the drake with his fist.

The woman's eyes softened for an instant, as though she were holding in laughter.

"No making fun of me," Deon said, gentling his voice. "I just rescued you."

He leaned down and hauled the woman over his shoulder. Before he could stop her, she darted one slim hand at the weapon, but she didn't try to grab it. She jabbed at a button and the red light turned green. Once that happened, she slumped against him in relief.

"I really need to figure out what this does," he said. "Come on, let's go home."

He laid her across the saddle of his growling drake, sprang aboard behind her and launched the drake across the plains toward the mountains.

Chapter Two
The Touch of a King

ೞ

They'd bound her hands.

Lea lay on a sofa in a huge room furnished with gold tables and chairs, her hands tied in front of her with a piece of leather. Next to the sofa, floor-to-ceiling windows opened to a mountain scene of incredible beauty and soft, sweet air wafted to her.

Across the room, a white-blond, godlike man picked over Lea's treasures. The black-haired man who'd rescued her stood with him, gesticulating as he spoke.

The black-haired man had blue beads braided into his hair and a tattoo of a lion hugging his bare right arm. His forehead bore a five-pointed star with the fifth point straight up. A pentacle, she thought it was called.

The white-blond man had red beads in his hair and was naked except for a piece of leather slung across his hips to cover his pertinent parts. His hair hung to his backside, but she could see when he moved that a lion tattoo covered his entire back. He had three pentacles on his forehead, each overlapping the other.

Every man and woman she'd seen as the black-haired man carried her through this palace had the pentacle tattoo somewhere on their bodies, plus some form of lion symbol. She was the only one she'd seen on this planet so far without a tattoo.

She must have been thrown severely off course when the harvester's fighters shot her down, because she'd sworn that the planet she'd fallen to didn't exist. She'd seen no record of it in any database or any star chart, and no way would the Four-

21

One-Six Empire pass up the chance to harvest a low-tech planet like this one.

Yet they remained untouched and unknown. How?

Her bonds were not tight enough to hurt, but she couldn't work herself free. Black Braids had at least been courteous enough to pull her torn flight suit over her bare breasts, though his grin indicated he thought it a shame to hide them. She wasn't certain that the shiver of warmth she'd felt had been entirely sane.

The two men were only curious about her for now and she hoped it stayed that way. She would not be able to fight if she had to, as banged up as she was. She probably had suffered all kinds of internal bleeding and would be dead before the night was through, in any case.

Cheerful thought. She was still in shock, still a little numb. From what she'd seen this place was both primitive and elegant, and she doubted these people had hospitals. The highest tech she'd seen so far was a block and tackle with carved wooden gears a man used to pile logs onto a two-wheeled oxen cart.

The two men looked over what her rescuer had brought back with him—her computerized ident card, her food, her anti-radiation dose, her pistol. Black Braids hadn't bothered with the bloodstone the falcon-man had taken, which made her think bloodstones were common here—he hadn't realized it was hers.

The white-blond man raised his head and said something to her. She wished she could understand him, because his voice was rich and full, caressing and soothing. Black Braids made a comment and laughed and the godlike man smiled at him.

And what a smile. It told her he carried a sadness inside him that he strove to hide, that he was fond of the man next to him and forgiving of his jokes and that he was interested in Lea but not in a bad way. At least not yet.

22

The godlike man spoke to her slowly and carefully. She shook her head. The two men exchanged a glance as though they were surprised and had no idea what to try next.

Lea let her head fall back on the sofa. She was far too tired to try to communicate. No technology, likely no meds and no machines to knit her insides back together again.

The white-blond man laid down her ident card and rubbed his fingers against his hip as though he needed to clean the technology from his skin. He approached her, his movements slow and careful, like he would an animal he didn't want to startle.

When he went down on one knee next to her, the impact of his physique hit her like a stun bolt. His bare thighs stretched tight, thick with muscle and covered with sinuous lion tattoos. Thank goddess the loincloth hung over his privates or she might have stared until her eyes popped out.

The thong that held the leather in place dipped to reveal coarse golden hair that started at his pelvis. More curls dusted his chest, covering a line of interlocked pentacle tattoos that led down his abdomen.

Across his throat he wore a silver pentacle on a leather thong. The silver looked pure and costly, incongruous hanging from the simple leather. His skin was sun-touched all over — no bathing suits for this man.

His face was square and handsome but not beautiful. He'd seen too much hardship and too much trouble for softness. This man was a fighter. His eyes were dark, like pools of blackness, his gaze holding her tighter than bonds.

She'd noticed that none of these people had colored eyes — they were all the darkest brown or black — and he studied her green eyes as though they were something exotic and strange.

His gaze drew her in, made her want to cup his cheek, to keep him looking at her as long as she could. His eyes held the wisdom of an old man, but he was young, probably about thirty years as Lea's people reckoned age.

He spoke to her slowly and softly, but she still had no idea what he said. Was it, *I'm going to touch you now, don't be afraid?* Or, *who are you and how do you want to die?*

He bent his head, pressing his hands together. His masculine scent was heady, his hair smelled of aloe and the ends of his braids brushed her leg, an erotic feeling though her skintight suit.

The white-blond man raised his head and placed his palms gently over her chest. For a moment she simply enjoyed the warmth of his touch, then she began to feel very strange.

His eyes widened like windows onto the night and her body rose to meet his without her say-so. She rested her bound hands on his strong shoulders and raised her face to him.

He turned his head so that his lips would just brush hers. She had no idea why she suddenly wanted to kiss him, a man who let his friend tie her up while he busily went through her possessions.

She felt strength humming through his hands and into her body. Her body responded, her heartbeat speeding, her blood pulsing, her temperature rising and her quim filling with warmth.

I'm going to have an orgasm, she realized. *I'm beat up, captured and tied with my clothes ripped open, and I want to have an orgasm.*

He kissed her again, another slow brush of lips. Her body wound higher, reaching toward climax, her hips lifting as she imagined his hard and huge cock rubbing her quim. Or perhaps in her mouth, her lips stretching around the tip.

Suddenly she realized he was *healing* her.

She gasped. Pain and exhaustion flowed from her like rivers in the spring, loosening her limbs and relaxing the terrified tightness inside her. She wanted to stretch and smile, no longer a hurt animal curling into a ball.

And she wanted to have sex with him. She glanced down at herself, grimy and bloody, her flight suit torn. Great. He was delectable and she looked like a street urchin.

She sat back, embarrassed, and he smoothed her hair from her face with a gentle hand.

"Thank you," she whispered.

His smile faded and his face took on a sudden look of pain, the tattoos on his brow creasing with his frown.

"Are you all right?"

He held his arm across his abdomen and bent his head, eyes closing.

Lea sat up, swinging her legs down. "Don't tell me you took my pain away but now you're feeling it."

She'd heard of empathic and telepathic healers who could transfer an injury to their own bodies, though she'd never seen one. The man pressed his hand to his face, as though he felt pretty crappy.

Black Braids strode across the room, his scowl fearsome. He growled something at the white-blond man, obviously angry. White-Blond looked up and answered, his deep voice weak and rasping, and Black Braids transferred his glare to Lea.

She gave him a helpless look. Black Braids stomped back across the room, rattled in an ornate cupboard that stood near the windows and returned with a goblet of blood-red liquid.

White-Blond raised his head as his friend shoved the goblet into his hand and he obediently downed the contents.

Black Braids snatched away the glass. White-Blond said something admonishing and returned his attention to Lea. He laid one hand on her brow, closed his eyes and began to speak in short, insistent phrases that churned in her brain.

At first it sounded like the same nonsense words, then gradually everything cleared, like static lifting to let a message through.

"...understand? I want you to understand me. Do you understand?"

"Yes," she gasped. "I do. How did you...?"

Black Braids puffed a sigh of relief. "Finally. Her gibberish was getting annoying."

"Your words sounded like gibberish to *me*," Lea pointed out.

White-Blond again held her gaze. "He is angry at me for expending my energy. But it was necessary. You were sorely hurt."

"After crashing? No big surprise."

"Another healer—" Black Braids began with a scowl.

"Might not have been strong enough," White-Blond interrupted. "She was dying."

"And you healed me," Lea said. "I guess it's no use asking how you did that."

Black Braids looked surprised. "He's the king."

Her gaze shot to White-Blond. "King?"

"All kings of Pamaar have the power to heal," White-Blond answered in his liquid-dark voice. "We heal the sickest and the most desperate and keep the land whole."

Black Braids started to say something else, but White-Blond stopped him. "It is done. This is Deon, my chief of arms, my protector." His voice and glance added, *my friend.* By the worried annoyance in Deon's eyes, Lea suspected their friendship was of the undying loyalty kind.

"I am Thane, leader of the lion-star clan and king of Pamaar. You came here in a falling star."

"A falling spaceship," she corrected him. "I was shot down. Good thing your planet turned out to be soft."

Deon frowned. "Planet?"

"Your world." She tapped the floor with her foot. "Pamaar, you called it."

After Thane and Deon exchanged a *what is she talking about?* look, Thane asked her, "Do you have a name?"

"Lea Auberge, flight lieutenant, second class."

"I've never heard of a clan with a long, unpronounceable name like that," Deon said.

"Just call me Lea—unless you plan to imprison and execute me. Then please use my full name."

Thane studied her curiously. "Executing you was not my intention. I want to find out about you and what your presence here means."

Deon leaned over her, his leather-clad body menacing. "What we want to know is if you've come here to murder Thane."

"I didn't know anything about Thane. Or this planet, until I started hurtling toward it. I didn't know it even existed. Or you." She looked at Thane. "But I'm glad you exist."

He raised a brow, probably wondering whether to be happy about that or not.

"It was pure luck I landed here." Lea thought regretfully of her lucky bloodstone stolen by the falcon-man. Maybe it *had* helped her. "Who was the man who found me? With the sword tattoos?"

"Felin, leader of the falcon-sword clan." Deon's voice held anger. "Thane's rival and sure to be sticking his ugly nose in soon."

"He stole my bloodstone."

Thane gave her a stilling look. "You wore a bloodstone?"

"Yes. My good luck charm. Why?"

"Bloodstones are sacred," Thane said. "If Felin has one…"

"Just what we need, a holy crusade," Deon growled. "Then again, if he can't prove he got it from a priestess, I can kill him. What a nice thought."

"Calm down. He might just put it under his pillow for good dreams. Why do you say it was luck that brought you here?" Thane asked Lea.

"Because I could easily have drifted around until my oxygen ran out. I was too far away for a rescue party and they knew it, the bastards. This planet caught my ship in its gravity, my ship was built well enough to keep me alive, I was captured by someone who can do psychic healing — you. Whether my luck continues remains to be seen."

"Did Felin hurt you?" Thane's voice went flat as he looked over her torn flight suit. "Tell me if he did."

"*Please.*" Deon smiled a not-nice smile. "Give me an excuse."

Lea shook her head. "He didn't paw me, but he didn't exactly look away either."

"I could beat on him a little," Deon offered.

"He will soon regret his actions." Thane's words were mild but his eyes held steel. "For now, I want you to consider yourself our honored guest," Thane continued. "I will provide whatever you wish — I imagine you'd like a bath and a rest."

"I'd love that." She raised her bound hands. "Honored guest?"

Thane nodded at Deon. Deon bent over her, brushing her with the scent of leather and male, then loosened the bonds and lifted them away.

"You're good at that," she remarked. "Tying people up, I mean."

The wicked grin Deon flashed her made her wish she'd phrased it a different way. She knew people on her planet who enjoyed typing-up games up with their mates, but never had she seen anyone smile like that about it. His smile said, *let me know when you want me to do it again.*

Thane broke in. "Anything you want, you have only to ask me or one of my servants — a meal, wine, sex."

She jumped. "Sex?"

Thane looked puzzled. "You do understand the word?"

"Yes. I meant—well, where I come from people don't automatically offer it to a guest."

Deon grunted. "Not very hospitable of them."

"A courtesan will be available to pleasure you," Thane explained in his deep voice. "Or two if you like. Do you prefer a man or a woman?"

"Both is always good," Deon added.

"*Courtesan.* Oh. I thought you meant *you* were offering…"

Thane looked surprised . "I would be happy to oblige if you like."

"Thane," Deon said in a warning tone.

"Deon is cautious, and wise to be." Thane clasped her fingers loosely. "I need to learn more about you and why you were sent to me."

"Yeah, I'd like to know that too."

Or at least why they thought so. And what she'd have to do to get back to the wreckage of her ship and see whether Felin and his men had left anything of it.

Hidden in a compartment above the pilot's chair was a tiny communications device that would tight-beam a distress signal to her people which would then home in on a sub-dermal implant behind her ear. No scout sent the normal, general distress signals when in trouble because those would only bring the Four-One-Six boys hard after them. The tight beam was to be used only when she had a definite location where she was stranded—or to locate her dead body. She hadn't had time or strength to get to the device before Felin had dragged her away.

Should she trust Thane and Deon with this information? She wasn't certain. Well, she was a scout and a good one, which meant she was expert enough to watch and learn while pretending not to.

Thane lifted her fingers to his lips. "After we talk, we might have sex. I would enjoy it."

I would too – oh gods, I would.

Even if this man and his sidekick decided to lock her up for good, she would love having sex with Thane. Just touching his body would be an orgasmic experience—he wouldn't even have to do anything.

Well, maybe he could do *something*…

"If there's any sex, count me in," Deon said to Thane. "I'm supposed to be protecting you anyway."

Lea gulped, remembering his sinful smile. *Does he mean one at a time or both together?*

Deon reached down and slid his fingers across Thane's shoulder. His touch was light, a caress.

And now we're going where I've never gone before. Some treacherous part of her added, *And wouldn't it be fun?*

Thane used Deon's arm to pull himself up. "My servants will see to your needs for now," he said.

It was a dismissal. Thane helped her to her feet, his arm rock-hard, his earlier weakness gone. At the same time, four people in simple garb, no less tattooed than Deon and Thane, entered and stood waiting at the door.

Of course Thane could afford to be polite and nice, she thought. He held all the cards. He had her, her ship was a wreck and he had confiscated her weapons and her identification.

Lea didn't have even a primitive map to show her where she was on this planet, no way to communicate with her people and no way to travel. Those dragon things Deon rode so fearlessly looked scary as hell. Their teeth were as long as her arm and no way was she approaching one on her own.

No, she was stuck in this beautiful palace with two tall, gorgeous men who offered to have sex with her as casually as they'd offer her a glass of wine.

Maybe she was still in her ship, unconscious and dreaming all this.

In that case, I'll sit back and enjoy it.

But she knew this was real, every minute of it, and she needed to figure out where she was and what was going on and what these two men wanted—besides sex.

As the polite servants led her out, Thane glanced up from the table. "Sleep well," he said in his gorgeous voice.

"Sure thing," she said, her body warming. She had a feeling she knew what she was going to dream about.

Chapter Three
Customs

ഇ

Thane heard Deon approach as he studied the woman's odd weapon at the table. He sensed his friend's agitation without looking up, and caught the scent of leather and Deon's spice.

"Be careful with that," Deon said. "Sliced that boulder right in half. Scared the shit out of me."

"It scared Felin too, you said."

"Yeah, he obviously didn't know what it could do. Damn good thing I got it away from him."

Thane carefully laid the metallic weapon next to the other accoutrements. The knife he understood, although its seamless and plain manufacturing puzzled him. All weapons on Pamaar were decorated and considered an art form. No artisan would craft a knife without his specific patterns emblazoned on the hilt or blade.

The square, shiny box he didn't understand and there was no way to open it. The same with the slender metallic tube.

Then there was the flatter box made of a similar shiny substance that could be pushed at one end. From the other end protruded a glob that looked orange and slightly disgusting, though he could see grains floating in it.

He sniffed it. "This is food, I think."

"Poison maybe."

"She's eaten some." One corner had been distinctly nibbled.

"Maybe she has the antidote."

Thane snorted a laugh. "My ever-suspicious bodyguard. I'm not going to eat it—I'm curious, that's all."

"I didn't see any tattoos on her." Deon slung his hip against the table and dangled his booted leg. "Haven't checked her entire body, of course."

"She'll undress to bathe. I'll have the servants tell me. Or the courtesans. I sent her one of each in case she changes her mind and wants release right away."

"How can she have no tattoos? Unless she had them removed, and who would do that?"

"She spoke no language familiar to me and I know every language of Pamaar," Thane mused, then he looked Deon in the eye. "We both know what we don't want to say, that she's from beyond the Warding."

Deon looked stricken. "That's impossible."

"You said you saw the wreckage of the fireball that brought her here—what did she call it? A *spaceship*."

"I've never heard of anything like that."

"Neither have I. We have to face that she came in through the Warding. And what's more, Felin will figure it out as well."

Thane traced Deon's swallow down his brown throat. Deon was a fighter, a warrior. He liked to solve problems with his sword and drink wine and laugh about it afterwards. He didn't like complex problems like Thane's waning powers and weakening Wards.

"You know the legends," Thane said. "When the Warding is gone, we will be devastated. There will be nothing to stop the outer darkness." He regarded the objects Lea had brought, small symbols of coming destruction.

"It isn't your fault," Deon said with heat. "A king's power shouldn't wane even when he is old unless there's something very wrong with him. And there's nothing wrong with you. You're virile as hell, I can attest."

"We don't know that it isn't my fault. I might have done something to weaken the Warding and possibly am making it worse by staying on."

"Don't you dare start asking me to kill you again. I'm not doing it."

Thane felt Deon's fear and worry rolling off him. Deon was loyal and would die for Thane but hated decisions that weren't black and white.

"Come here." He tugged Deon closer by his tunic and Deon slid his hand to Thane's waist.

"I never would have survived this long without you beside me," Thane said, his face an inch from Deon's.

"Or in front of you, or behind you."

"I wasn't forgetting."

Their lips gently met. Deon snaked his tongue into Thane's mouth, tasting of sharp spice. He threaded his fingers behind Thane's long hair, holding the nape of his neck as they kissed.

Thane let his fingers travel to the large bulge between Deon's thighs. Deon moved his feet apart, letting Thane stroke. Thane's own cock was already as hard, reacting to feeling his friend ready and randy.

"You like that girl, don't you?" Deon asked. "I heard the glee in your voice when she said she wanted to have sex with you."

"Did I sound that eager?"

"You sounded that horny. She's sweet, I agree. No matter what her part is in all this, I say we take her to bed. I won't be able to watch over you if I don't join in."

"Right. Your protective instinct."

"You betcha."

"*When the star falls, the queen will come and the world will be reborn.* We've had the falling star and a woman. Now to see what the seer meant by the world being reborn."

"Maybe we don't want to know," Deon said.

"Maybe not. But for right now…" He licked Deon's cheek.

Deon slid his hand to Thane's ass, loosening the thong that held the loincloth in place. "Don't you have a kingdom to run?"

"It can wait twenty minutes."

Deon gave him a stare of mock outrage. "Twenty minutes? What do you take me for?"

"My most loyal friend."

"You got that right." He tossed Thane's loincloth aside and pressed his warm hand under Thane's balls. "What do you want first?"

Thane grew harder as Deon's sleek black hair brushed his chest. "Your mouth. I want your mouth on me."

Deon grinned and drew his tongue across Thane's lower lip. "Hang onto something."

Thane gripped the edge of the table with one hand as Deon sank to his knees, leather brushing Thane's heated skin. Thane made a noise of satisfaction as his friend closed his mouth over his very ready cock.

Deon had a gifted tongue and he plied it well. He rubbed the underside of Thane's penis with it all the way to his balls, finding every spot of fiery ecstasy. Thane's fingers bit the table until he thought they'd indent the wood.

Then Deon sucked. Thane looked down to see Deon's eyes closed, his cock disappearing beyond his lover's lips, the stiff shaft pressing the inside of Deon's cheek. Deon grunted a little with concentration and Thane's balls lifted and tightened.

"Damn, you suck good," he whispered.

Deon looked up and smiled around the huge cock in his mouth.

Thane clenched his fists and suddenly his seed shot out of him and onto Deon's waiting tongue.

Fuck it, he'd wanted to spin it out, have Deon suck him for a long time before Thane couldn't stand it anymore and demanded his ass. But Thane was pent up from meeting Lea and from the connection he'd made when he healed her. She'd almost climaxed with it and he'd wanted so bad to screw her right then while Deon watched. Only caution had kept him away from her, forcing him to offer her courtesans instead.

Deon's throat moved as he swallowed Thane down, his lips wet with Thane's semen.

"Fucking damn," he rumbled, easing away and wiping his mouth. "You needed that."

"How did you know?" Thane's body was still hot, his adrenaline pumping. The release hadn't eased his need — it had only made him hotter.

He pulled Deon to his feet and laced his tongue into the other man's mouth, sliding his hands to his leather-clad ass. He loved how Deon tasted with himself and Deon all mixed up, evidence of their sacred-bond.

"There's no one here but us," Thane said.

He knew Deon would understand what he meant. His friend's eyes darkened. "No."

They had this argument all the time. "I need it. I don't know how much longer I'm going to be alive — give me that at least."

"No." Deon put his hand on Thane's chest but didn't push him away. "I can't and you know it. Don't ask me."

"I can order you to, as your king."

"You can order me to jump off the highest tower, too, and I'll do that before I'll let you break the laws of Pamaar. Stupid laws, but nonetheless."

"I know it's bad when you use a word like *nonetheless*."

"Hey, I can read a dictionary too."

"You need to release," Thane said. That was obvious—the lacings of Deon's leggings bowed outward with the pressure of his wanting.

"That's all right. I can call a courtesan. Balin is around somewhere."

Thane stepped away to catch his breath, trying not to argue any more. Deon was right—they had to follow the rules, as much as it killed them, now more than ever. "Come here," he said quietly. "I can touch you at least."

Deon tugged the bellpull anyway and spoke in a soft voice to the servant who cracked open the door. Then Deon came to Thane and let Thane unlace his leggings and release his cock.

Deon was hard and heavy, warm goodness in Thane's hand. He kissed Deon, mostly to keep him from starting the argument again, while he stroked Deon's hot, swollen shaft. Thane loved the feel of it, fat and long, the tip satin-soft. It would feel so good filling his ass, if only...

Balin entered and Thane stepped away. Balin was a courtesan, with sleek brown hair and interlaced tattoos running along the insides of his arms. He took in Deon standing, scowling and hard, and Thane, who sank to the nearest divan, spreading his legs to cool off. Balin's look turned questioning and Thane gave him a silent nod.

Balin stripped off, revealing a tall, hard body, and Thane got to watch while Deon worked him up, slathering him with lube. Then Balin got down on all fours on the carpeted floor with Deon hard and ready behind him.

"Thane," Deon groaned as he slid inside.

Balin turned his head and looked over at Thane with an expression of understanding. Deon threw his head back and pumped hard into Balin's ass. "Thane," he moaned again. "Damnation, I love you..."

* * * * *

The bath was a thing of luxury, a gold-plated tub seven feet long and four feet deep, filled to the brim with steaming water. One of the female servants remained with Lea to help strip away her flight suit and ease her in.

As Lea sat back in the welcoming water, the woman looked over the flight suit in curiosity, examining the fire-retardant, radiation-blocking material and running her hands along the nearly invisible seams.

"It's strong like silk but feels like linen," the maid said. "Is it flax?"

"No, it's… Well, I'm not sure how to explain, I just know it protects me from fire and too much battering."

"What clan grows the crop to make it? Or is it from an animal, like a goat?"

"It's artificial," Lea said, closing her eyes as the bathwater's heat bit into her muscles. "Made in a factory. I use it but don't really know much about how it's made."

"Artificial," the maid repeated. "I do not know this word."

"Artificial means not real. Or at least manufactured, not natural."

"Not real?" The maid turned surprised eyes to the flight suit. "But I am holding it, so it is real. How can a thing be not natural?"

"Now we're delving into philosophy. Maybe I'd better stick to getting clean."

"Of course." The maid folded the torn flight suit and put it on a chair. "I talk too much, but I am a curious lady. I will scrub your back."

Lea had never had anyone scrub her back except the occasional cute man she took shore leave with, but the maid brought out a huge sponge and a loofah as big as Lea's head and started to rub Lea down. After a moment of resistance, Lea gave in to the pleasure of having the dirt and sweat rubbed from her skin.

She was even happier to be dried off with big towels and dressed in a soft silk robe that clung to her skin. The maid led her to a bedroom with a huge bed strewn with cushions. Lea, used to her bunk back at the barracks or sleeping in a cramped ship, found it strange to sink among so many pillows. The maid even tucked her in.

"Thane is the king," Lea said, trying to fight sleep until she understood a few things. "But he seems unhappy. Did something bad happen to him?"

The maid's expression became guarded. "His wife died a few years back. She was a good woman."

"Oh I'm sorry. Does he have children?"

More caution. "No."

"That's too bad." A king with no children, if she remembered her archaic Earth history correctly, could be in a dangerous situation because there would be no heir. Someone else—she remembered the hard face of the falcon-man who'd pulled her out of the ship—might try to step in.

She yawned as the maid straightened the covers. The woman wore a simple sleeveless tunic, baring strong arms with tiny pentacle tattoos. "And you are part of this pentacle clan?"

"Lion-star," the woman said. "Yes. We all are. We are the ruling clan this cycle."

"This cycle?"

"Four cycles, four clans. When Thane dies, long may he live, the next clan will take up the kingship."

"Let me guess, the falcons."

"The falcon-sword clan. And then the dragon-wand clan and the tiger-vessel clan."

Lea began to slide into sleep. "Pentacles, swords, wands, vessels—cups, maybe? Like the Tarot?"

"The what?"

"Cards," Lea murmured. "It's in the cards."

39

Suspicion entered the maid's voice. "You should have been taught all about clans as a child. Which clan did the king say you were from?"

Lea's dimming awareness advised caution. "I hit my head pretty hard. I don't remember things."

Instantly the maid's touch became solicitous. "No more questions. You sleep well now. The king has touched you, so you'll get better."

Lea remembered Thane's warm hands, the darkness of his eyes that pulled her in, in, in. She remembered how her body had heated, spiraling into ecstasy. "Mmm, maybe he can touch me again."

"Not just now." The maid plumped another pillow. "You need rest and he is with Lord Deon."

Lea cracked open her eyes. "When you say *with*, do you mean..." Remembering Deon's caress and Thane's reaction, she made a circle with her thumb and forefinger and pierced it with her other forefinger.

The maid stared at her blankly. "Of course."

"They're lovers?"

"Yes." The maid obviously had no idea why she was asking. "Have been since they came of age. They're sacred-bonded."

"I thought you said the king had been married."

"Yes."

"And he was lovers with Deon?"

"When the king married, Lord Deon became the queen's lover as well. As it should be."

"Not where I come from," Lea said under her breath.

"Perhaps you don't remember," the maid said, trying to sound reassuring. "Now, you go to sleep. Maybe your memories will come back when you awake."

Lea closed her eyes again, knowing she needed the rest to face whatever was to come. "Honored guest" might be Thane's way of saying "prisoner" in this gilded cage.

He and Deon? She imagined the two hard-bodied men touching each other. Their arms around one another, tongues probing each other's mouths. Cocks long and hard and swollen, Thane's in Deon's mouth.

A shiver racked her body and her quim filled. She put her hand down to press against it, and to that sensation she fell into deep sleep.

* * * * *

She woke to someone stroking her hair. She thought of Thane's handsome face and night-dark eyes, and purred against the touch in her half-sleep.

"Mmm. Thane."

"Do I look like Lord Thane to you?" a voice filled with humor said. A woman's voice.

Lea snapped her eyes open. A lush woman lay next to her, late afternoon sunlight touching hair of deep red that flowed in ringlets over the curve of her waist.

She wore a blue silk robe open to her navel and had small and intricate lion and pentacle tattoos on her cheekbones. A line of twined flowers decorated the insides of her arms under the loose sleeves of the robe.

Lea threw off covers and scrambled to the other side of the bed, landing on her knees, eyes wide. The woman gave her a puzzled look.

"Is something wrong?"

"You're a woman," Lea gasped.

She laughed, her dark eyes crinkling. "I know that. My name is Emilie. Thane sent me."

"He *sent* you? But I don't—not with women."

Emilie didn't look in the least worried. "He wasn't certain. It is no trouble if you prefer a man." She rolled off the bed and sauntered to the door, the silk robe clinging to her hips.

She opened the door to admit a man as attractive as Emilie but in no way effeminate. He had thick brown hair gathered in a tail, a square, masculine face and a firm body under a tight, sleeveless tunic. The same kind of interlinked flower pattern Emilie had flowed down the insides of his arms.

He had dark eyes like Thane and Deon, but they held nowhere near the sadness of Thane or the wariness of Deon. He was a man who lived for sensual pleasure and his smile told her so.

"This is Balin," Emilie said. "Lea says she prefers a man."

"Lucky for me," Balin answered. He had a rich, deep voice, not quite the dark timbre of Thane but not bad.

Lea realized they expected her to accept Balin as a substitute for Thane and be happy about it. "Wait."

Balin looked surprised. "All right." He sat down on the edge of the bed, completely at his ease. "You tell me when you're ready."

She shook her head in disbelief. "Holy goddess, you people really know how to take someone prisoner."

"Prisoner?" Emilie asked blankly and Balin looked equally perplexed.

"Never mind. I need to see Thane. I'm awake now and feel much better. I really need to talk to him." *And try to figure out if I can retrieve my pistol and get back to my ship to call for help.*

"You cannot at present," Emilie said. "The king is with Lord Deon."

"*Still?*" Good gods, they had stamina.

"Still?" Emilie repeated.

"They were together when I went to sleep. It's late afternoon now—I must have been asleep for hours."

"You have been asleep for two and a half days," Balin said. "We've been waiting for you to wake up. Lord Thane wanted us to be here in case you wanted pleasuring when you came out of sleep."

"Two and a half..." Lea put her hand to her tangled hair. "Sweet gods, why didn't anyone wake me? My ship's been laying out there two and a half days. I need..."

Emilie put her hand on Lea's shoulder. Balin likewise stroked the fold of her thigh, both touches soothing. "You needed to heal," Emilie said. "Lord Thane told us you were sore hurt, near to dying. He started the healing process but your body needs rest to complete it."

"And he provided me with someone willing to have sex with me in case I wanted it when I woke up," Lea finished, dazed. "How thoughtful of him." *Keeping me sated so I won't run away.*

"Yes." Emilie looked pleased she understood. "If you prefer Balin only that will be fine, or we could both pleasure you if you like."

"Does everyone on this planet hop into bed with everyone else? What about STDs?"

Balin and Emilie exchanged a glance. "STDs?" Balin ventured.

"Sexually transmitted diseases." When they looked baffled again, she said impatiently, "You know, you have sex with someone and they have a virus and pretty soon everyone has it."

Emilie shook her head. "I have never heard of such a thing. We have no disease here. We have the king."

"The walking pharmacy?"

They had no idea what she was talking about. "These words," Emilie said. "Lord Thane gave you knowledge of our language, but I think it did not work all the way."

"Let me get this straight. There is no disease here because the minute anyone gets a cough, the king cures you?"

43

The glance the two courtesans exchanged this time was more cautious. "Yes."

"How can he be so many places at once?"

"The king has the healing power of the land," Balin explained. "He can charge others to heal in his name. He did so with his queen, who was a great healer, and with others of the clan. Few fall ill. The land keeps us whole."

If that's true, why did Thane's wife die? she wondered. An accident perhaps, like a fall—or maybe one of those fire-drakes had chomped on her. Would these two tell her? But they looked at each other warily now, as though advising care in their words.

"All right, so you have sex without fear of some embarrassing or deadly illness. But what about marriage? You take husbands and wives here, right? The maid who put me to bed said that when the king married, Deon became the queen's lover too."

The pair of them nodded without surprise.

"So you exchange partners and have courtesans without anyone being upset?"

Emilie laughed. "Men and women who marry share great love."

Balin continued, "If they want other partners in the mix and both of them love the third or fourth party, then no one is unhappy. And everyone calls for courtesans. Sometimes a husband brings one in for his wife and himself for fun. As long as it is done in love and with consent, no one minds."

"I can't believe this planet has stayed hidden this long," Lea said half to herself. "If everyone knew what a sexual paradise was here, they'd go on shore leave and never come back."

Emilie and Balin were giving each other that *she's crazy but humor her* look again.

"What about children?" Lea asked. "With sex comes children, and if you're freely promiscuous you must be overrun with children."

"What is wrong with children?" Balin asked. "I have my two."

"I have one so far," Emilie said, her eyes lighting with pride. "A beautiful daughter."

"Yes, but... Surely these husbands and wives who bring in extra partners and courtesans whenever they want have many more children than two. Unless you all have a hell of a birth control program."

"Every woman has two children," Emilie said, her voice gentle. "When they are ready."

"Only two? And you can choose when to be pregnant?"

She nodded. "Yes. You must know that."

Lea remembered the maid's surprise that she didn't know about the clans, and her own feeble explanation that she'd hit her head. The maid had probably explained that the poor, beat-up woman in the king's guest room had gone out of her mind.

"Sure. I know that." She trailed off, deciding to curb her curiosity. She needed to know everything she could about these people if she were to keep herself safe, but apparently Thane wanted them to think she was from this planet.

Plus she had no idea whether they could secretly pipe information to the empire that they'd caught a rogue scout from the Rock. She hadn't seen any advanced technology so far, but that didn't mean they didn't have it hidden.

"I need to get up," Lea said. She swung her legs around the side of the bed, but suddenly Emilie was behind her, soothing hands on her shoulders. Emilie's fingers found muscles that were stiff from Lea lying in bed two and a half days and eased them loose.

"You are still fatigued. I see it in your face."

Balin placed a warm hand on her abdomen. His smile had become promising, his eyes dark.

"I want to talk to Thane," she said, her voice faint.

"He is with Lord Deon," Emilie repeated. "In counsel."

"Is that what they're calling it these days?"

"They have many matters to discuss," Emilie said.

Balin twined his fingers through the backs of hers. "In the meantime, let's see how you taste." He lifted her hand and licked her palm. "Mmm. Very nice. Now lie back and let me taste your quim."

Lea swallowed. "Taste my..."

"If you like," Emilie said in soft voice, "you can lick my pussy while he goes down on you. Would you like that?"

Gods have mercy. Lea shouldn't be excited by sex talk from another woman, but her nipples pinched hard and heat began to leak between her thighs. These two knew exactly what to say and in exactly what tone of voice.

"Thank you, but—"

"If you are not comfortable with that, I can suckle you instead," Emilie offered. "Many women like that. Or I can simply watch."

Lea let out a groan. This could not be happening to her. It would be so easy to succumb while Balin kissed her cheek and whispered that he wanted to drink the nectar between her thighs. But she had to remain on guard and find out what Thane intended to do with her, and whether she could get back to her ship.

"Really, I want to see Thane."

Balin smiled. "I cannot fault your taste. He is a fine man."

"Don't tell me—you're his lover too?"

"When he and Lord Deon wish it. And they like Emilie. We are at the top of the courtesan class and are often called to please the king. He specifically requested us for you."

"Like offering someone the best bottle of wine," she said.

"Exactly." Balin seemed pleased she understood.

"Lie back," Emilie said gently. Balin moved off the bed and slid the silk up Lea's legs. His thumbs found the swollen nub of her clit.

"Ah, she is ready," Balin said. "And very wet."

Lea watched Emilie's nipples draw to dark points. "That is good," Emilie whispered.

Sweet gods, I'm about to be pleasured by a courtesan sent to me by the king I have the hots for. No one is going to believe my report. She thought about Justin, her closest friend in the fleet. They'd never been lovers, but he was the only one she could talk about sex with and vice versa.

She could almost hear his grating voice, *So you got your rocks off with male courtesan, eh? Whoa kid.*

She felt a sharp pain in her heart, missing him and fearing she'd never see Justin again. But no, he would have started looking for her by now. Would a search party find her on this world that appeared on no charts?

"You are worried," Emilie told her.

"You could say that."

"For this moment, troubles do not exist," Balin said. His eyes were dark like Thane's had become when he'd healed her. "Let me pleasure you with my fingers, then my tongue, then my cock. If you wish to pretend I am Lord Thane, you may. Feel free to call me by his name."

"Wouldn't that be rude?"

"Not at all. I am here to pleasure you. That is what I am for."

"And if I say no, I don't want any?"

"Then we stop." Balin kept his face neutral but she saw disappointment in his eyes. "We truly only wish to make you feel good."

47

His fingers softly rubbing her clit certainly felt good. She moaned again without meaning to.

"Why do you fight your desires?" Emilie asked. "It's not healthy for you."

"Is he trying to torture me? Or test me?"

"Who?" Balin asked, confused.

"Thane."

Balin laughed. "He does not call this torture. If you do prefer to be tied up, we can send for the courtesans who do this. Lord Deon is good at it and he will know the best of those who specialize in bondage."

"Deon is into bondage? I should have guessed with all the black leather he wears."

"He wears leather for riding and fighting," Emilie said, confused again. "It is protective. When he plays, he usually likes to be naked."

Lea had a sudden vision of Deon, the powerful black-haired warrior, stark naked and asking with a sinful smile if Lea was ready for him.

Balin's fingers, which hadn't stopped, burned on her clit. She added to the vision Thane, equally as naked, watching Deon. The fantasy coupled with Balin's light touch triggered her orgasm.

She writhed and bumped against the bed in a wave of sudden ecstasy while Emilie smiled, looking happy. Balin teased her for a while longer then leaned down and pressed a kiss to her swollen nub.

"Mmm, you do taste like honey."

"Sweet gods, I didn't mean to do that," she panted

A voice rolled from the other side of the room, "I hope you did."

Lea gasped and sat up. The two courtesans rose from the bed, bowing respectfully. "My lord," Balin said.

Thane stood in the doorway, white-blond hair tousled to his waist, his dark eyes taking in everything. Behind him was Deon, dark and warrior-like, enjoying the scene.

Lea got hastily to her knees and pulled her robe closed, blushing hard. "Thane," she said hoarsely. "Hello."

Chapter Four
Drakes vs. Spacecraft

Thane found everything about Lea fascinating. Her hair was four different shades of gold all tangled together and silky to the touch. Courtesans often dyed their hair, but no dye of this world could match Lea's strange golden hue.

And her eyes were green. No one of Pamaar had green eyes — Lea's were lovely light green with flecks of gold, framed with golden lashes.

The ripped and stained garment she'd been found in had given him a glimpse of her delights, but the body-clinging silk robe she wore now showed every luscious curve of her. Her nipples pressed the silk in hard little nubs, betraying her excitement, and she couldn't quite hold the fabric closed over her thighs.

She had a siren's beauty, those legendary creatures that lured men to their deaths, and the best part was, she had no idea of this. If she had been an ordinary woman from the lion-star clan, he'd have laughed in delight, spread himself on the bed and said, *Have yourself a good time, darling.*

But she was a stranger from no clan at all, from beyond the Warding, and she should not be here. The maid who'd helped her undress and bathe had reported that Lea had no tattoos anywhere on her body.

Having no tattoos was unheard of. She was as undecorated as her plain knife, which made her very odd and very dangerous.

Deon caught his unspoken hint that he wanted to speak to Lea away from the courtesans. He gave Thane the barest nod, then caught Balin around his hips and towed Emilie toward him by her belt. Both courtesans smiled and melted against him.

Lea watched them with her lips parted, still kneeling on the bed. "You sent them to me."

"They are the best of their class," Thane answered. "Did you like them?"

"Really—I don't need sex."

The answer surprised him, because everyone needed sex. You could not have life without sex and frankly, he wouldn't want to.

"I need it," Deon rumbled. "Join in if you want."

He took the two courtesans to the other side of the large room and Lea's eyes widened as Deon slid his hands inside Emilie's robe and began to kiss her. Balin stripped off his tunic, the lion tattoo across his shoulders blending with the intricate courtesan tattoos on the underside of his arms.

"They're going to do it right in front of us," Lea said in amazement.

"Yes, why wouldn't they? Deon is my personal guard, and he'd hardly leave me alone with you so he could have sex."

"I'm not dangerous," she said, but her eyes shifted. "That crash beat me up and apparently I slept for two days and some change. I'm weak as a kitten."

He wished that not being able to understand half of what she said didn't make her so desirable. "Tell me about your...*spaceship*."

Again, her gaze flickered. "Not much to tell. A standard scout model XXH-2736, out three years ago, a good little ship that never needs much maintenance. Of course, you'd know that just looking at her—she's pretty common. No secrets."

Her words were glib, but Thane knew there was much more here than she revealed. He stretched out next to her on the bed, though she remained a little ball of blue silk on top of the pillows.

Thane wore only his loincloth and lying full-length, propped up on one elbow, would allow her to see all of him. She was trying not to look, but her gaze kept sweeping over him and lingering on his pelvic region.

"Ships float on the sea," he said. "But yours would sink."

"You've seen it then?"

"Deon and I flew out to it."

She looked alarmed then masked her expression. "On one of those dragon things? What are those? They can't be for real."

"I'd rather talk about your ship," he said firmly. "And where it came from."

"Space. Hence the name *spaceship*." She hesitated. "You can't be a low-tech world. You'd have been harvested by now. No one escapes the Four-One-Six."

"The *fouronesix*?"

"Unless you're working with them. That would be highly unusual, but I suppose it could happen — *oh Goddess*."

Thane looked around for the cause of her shock, but only saw that Deon had stripped. Emilie and Balin knelt in front of him and began licking his cock, their tongues tangling around each other's as they played. The sight made Thane harden himself.

Lea's face was cherry-red, but the sight obviously excited her. Her breasts tightened and he smelled her arousal.

"Do not be embarrassed by desire." Thane rested his hand on her thigh, liking the smooth silk of her robe. "It is a joyous thing, a celebration of life."

"Well, they sure look like they're celebrating."

Deon closed his eyes and tilted his head back. Thane always liked watching Deon in pleasure — the man sank himself into it. Balin and Emilie had been wise choices to become royal courtesans because they knew exactly how much to give and when to back off, when it was time for games and when Deon and Thane wanted to be alone.

"The courtesans are highly skilled," Thane said. "Balin has been chosen as the only man allowed to enter the king."

Her shocked gaze flicked from the threesome to Thane. "I'm sorry? Did you say *enter* the king?"

"He has been given clearance to, should I desire it. A man must be highly trusted to do that. Only in Deon's presence, of course."

"But I thought you and Deon…"

"Are lovers? We are. But the king's personal bodyguard, by law, is not allowed to enter him. There is the danger that the king would become too highly influenced by him—at least that's what the law says. I'd trust Deon with my life and I think I could fall under his sway even without him penetrating me, but the king must respect the laws. We find many ways to enjoy ourselves, in any case."

She listened, openmouthed. "I can't believe I'm having this conversation."

"I can't believe you know nothing of what I'm telling you. Where do you truly come from, what clan? And why did you remove your tattoos?"

"I've never had tattoos. For one thing, in spaceflight, you never know when you're going to run through a heavily magnetic area and if there's metal in the ink, you're kind of screwed. Besides, I have a thing about needles."

"Tattoos never hurt."

"Why? Because you're there to heal everyone's pain?"

"Tattoos are done by the very best artists and they receive the king's healing powers."

"I see."

She closed her mouth again, shutting her curiosity behind her eyes. He sensed that every question she asked masked what she truly wanted to know. Nor was she going to tell him what *he* truly wanted to know.

"What about my stuff? My ration bar and knife and things."

"They are safe," he assured her. "Locked away in my rooms. No one will take them."

She bit her lip as though she didn't like his answer. "I want to see my ship."

"It is nothing but a ruined heap, mostly burned."

"I want to see it anyway. Or is that your way of telling me I'm not allowed to leave your palace?"

He shrugged. "I will take you to see it, on one condition."

"And that is?"

She looked wary, like a hunted animal. He wanted to explain that he kept her here for her protection, so Felin wouldn't find her and use her, but he also knew Deon wasn't completely wrong to advise caution. They had no idea who she was or where she came from or who she worked for—or what danger to Pamaar she represented.

He rose to his knees and reached for her, cupping his hands around her face. "Let me give you another healing."

Her lips parted and her eyes focused on his, the pupils spreading black through the green. He felt her pulse beneath his fingers, her breath on his face. She had a cleanness about her, a sparkling honesty that wove through her aura.

He traced the pain of her injuries, faint now, down to the root of them, to find them mostly healed. Thane needed only a small dose of his power to further close the wounds and erase the faint scars they left behind. The pain to himself was small, though he couldn't stop his a small intake of breath as he felt the pull.

"It hurts you," she said, sounding distressed.

He nodded, but her compassion tugged at his heart. He closed his eyes and let their lips meet.

Holy gods. She was ripe and sweet and *damn* she tasted good.

Her breath came fast, warming his skin. It was easy to push her down into the bed, to lay full-length over her and feel her lush body against his. He kissed her again, sliding his hand inside her robe and catching the globe of her breast in his palm.

Across the room, the sounds of sex became more intense but Thane had no desire to turn his head to see what they were up to. Looking into Lea's eyes was more pleasurable for now.

"Is this payment for you taking me to my ship?" she murmured.

He smiled, feeling genuine mirth for the first time in a long time. "That is a fun idea, but no. This is entirely voluntary."

He kissed her again, plucking her nipple between his fingers, liking how she rose to his touch. His cock was hard and tight, and he rubbed her quim through the thin layers of cloth separating him from her.

He heard Deon cry out, "Oh gods, *fuck,* I'm coming."

Hearing his friend so happy made Thane warm with need. He kissed Lea, letting his hand open the robe further and move to her quim.

"You're beautiful," he whispered. "And so wet." He drew his hand away and tasted her on his fingertips. "Do you need to release?"

"I'd say so." Her voice was a throaty rasp.

Thane looked up to where Deon had collapsed to a chair, holding both courtesans on his lap while they kissed him.

"Deon, my friend. I have need of you."

He felt Lea gasp as Deon gently put Emilie and Balin aside and walked across the room, still naked, his cock already rising. He had a lion tattoo across his pelvis that moved sinuously as he strolled to them.

He looked at Lea in her half-open robe, eyes sparkling. "What do you need?" He sat down on the bed and ran a caressing hand over Lea's leg. "Would you like me to take her, or watch while you fuck her?"

Lea suddenly rolled out from under Thane and faced them on her knees again, hands out. "All right, wait a minute. Him *watching*? I'm not used to any of this."

Deon looked slightly surprised but not offended. "It's way too dangerous to let him lie in a lover's arms without me looking out for him. But I'd be happy to oblige if you want release."

"Release? Is that all it is?" She sounded disappointed, which intrigued Thane.

Deon grinned. "We *need* to release—what's wrong with enjoying it?"

"Obviously I can't explain," Lea said, her face red.

Deon shrugged, always easygoing about sex. He ran light fingers across Thane's cheekbone. "Do *you* need me?"

"Not right now," Thane said gently. "At least let me release you, Lea. It's not good to hold it in."

"Maybe she could do it herself," Deon suggested. "I wouldn't mind seeing that."

Thane wouldn't either. He imagined Lea kneeling on the bed, her robe open, while her fingers played between her legs. He would stroke her back, encouraging her, while she stroked her warm, wet center. She'd moan softly with it then withdraw her fingers, glistening with dew, and raise them to his lips.

But he knew that wouldn't happen right this minute. Her chest rose and fell as though she shared the vision with him, but she seemed embarrassed and awkward instead of eager. That must be it—they were all looking at her the way they'd view an unusual flower or new kind of art, which had to be unnerving. But she was so different, so unique, he couldn't help but stare.

"We can wait until later," Thane told her gently. "After I show you your ship." He turned to Deon. "Prepare your drake to take us back out to the valley where she fell from the sky."

From the flick of Deon's eyes, Thane knew he wanted to ask a sharp *why?* but he kept his thoughts to himself. He also kept quiet his disappointment that the sexual play wouldn't continue.

Lea's eyes widened. "Oh geez, now *they're...*"

Across the room Balin lay on his back on the floor, his hands tucked behind his head, while Emilie happily rode him.

Deon chuckled. "We wound them up pretty tight, you and me. They deserve some enjoyment."

"*I* did?" Lea's green eyes widened in amazement.

"Emilie told me you didn't want them. They forgive you because they know you're tired and hurt and don't mean to be rude."

"It's rude to turn down sex?"

"To a courtesan it is," Deon said. "It's like telling the best artist in the world that you really *don't* want the sculpture she made especially for you."

"Oh."

Thane smiled at her, trying to look reassuring. "Leave her be, Deon. She doesn't understand."

Why she didn't understand was the mystery. She didn't know concepts taught to Pamaaran children in every clan from the earliest age. He exchanged another glance with Deon that warned his partner not to pry too much and put her on her guard. Coaxing information from a person was much easier and more rewarding than threatening them.

He had no intention of having Lea look at him in fear and every intention of her looking at him in desire. She almost trusted him, was almost ready to surrender to him, but not quite.

He hoped by the end of the day to make that surrender complete.

* * * * *

"Do we really have to ride on that thing?"

Lea peered in trepidation at the dragon-like creature that waited in the courtyard. It stood calmly tethered to a thick pole, a wide saddle on its back, but it was a far cry from the docile farm horses on Lea's planet.

The drake stood ten feet high at its shoulder, the neck extending beyond that. Its leathery wings were folded against its body, but she'd seen its wingspan out in the valley, not to mention felt the strength of the creature herself.

Deon laughed, voice rumbling and deep. "You aren't afraid of Cutie are you? He's gentle as a puppy."

"A five-ton puppy," Lea muttered darkly.

Deon found her hilarious, but Thane put a warm hand on her shoulder. He'd donned a gray tunic and breeches tucked into black boots and thrown a gray cloak over it all, like an adventurer in the books she'd read as a child. A tightly muscled, leather-booted, gorgeous adventurer with sin-dark eyes.

"I'll be with you," he said. "You'll be all right."

Thane had an amazing ability to make her feel hopeful and assured. When he'd started to kiss her on the bed, she'd been ready to hump him then and there, no matter that he held her virtual prisoner, no matter who else was in the room. The courtesans and Deon hadn't been paying attention anyway.

When Thane had asked Deon to watch, she'd snapped out of her wanting. Thane wasn't a man she'd met on shore leave who'd agreed to have casual—safe, of course—sex with her before she had to report back.

Thane was king of his country and he lived in a palace with a fearsome guardsman who was also his lover, and they'd captured Lea, no matter what a nice spin Thane put on it. He didn't trust her and she didn't know if she could trust him.

He'd locked away her accoutrements and she wondered what excuse he'd make if she asked to see them. Not that she cared about her tasteless rations or even her ident card, but her pistol would feel good next to her hip.

But she knew without asking that he wouldn't let her have the gun. Deon had witnessed how dangerous it was and no matter how much Thane offered her food and drink and sex, he wasn't stupid enough to let her run around armed.

Ergo, a clean, fun relationship was not possible here. She needed to find her spaceship, send a signal and get the heck off this planet.

Several servants came out to the courtyard to hold the drake while they mounted. Deon scrambled to the saddle without assistance and reached down for Lea. Thane lifted her into Deon's arms, then he hauled himself up using Deon's hand for balance.

One of the servants tossed the reins to Deon and with a sudden, sickening jolt, the drake launched itself into the sky.

Lea squeezed her eyes shut and clung to the saddle's ropes. The drake didn't fly smoothly—he swooped and glided and dropped and rose until Lea gritted her teeth.

"It's all right." Deon's voice warmed her ear. "I'm right behind you. And Thane's behind me. Right where I like him."

Lea peeled open her eyes to find a landscape of incredible beauty floating below her. They'd left the city, which receded to a glittering pile on the horizon. Instead of steel skyscrapers, turrets of stone lined the city walls like intricate lace, looking like fairy-tale palaces Lea had read of as a child.

No smudge of pollution or dust hung over the planet and blue sky arched softly overhead. Razor-sharp mountains sliced the horizon to the left of the city, but to its right, where the drake flew, were rolling hills and green swards. She saw cultivated fields with roads running neatly through them and clusters of thatch-roofed houses. She'd glimpsed some of this when Deon had flown her to the palace, but she'd been injured and out of it and hadn't been able to fully appreciate it until now.

"It's beautiful," she breathed.

"It's home," Thane said from behind Deon, but his voice held sadness.

They flew for nearly an hour, while the green landscape rolled under them, then Deon jerked the reins and Lea bit back a yelp as the drake plummeted sharply. The emerald turf of the valley to which they glided was marred by a long black streak that ended in a tangle of charred metal.

Deon landed the drake with barely a bump and Thane dismounted. He reached up and lifted Lea down, then Deon swung his leg over the drake's neck and dropped to the ground beside them.

Lea walked to the wreckage in sorrow. "She was such a good little ship. Those bastards are going to pay."

She sensed Deon and Thane behind her and knew she wouldn't get much chance to act. She knelt in the small cockpit, the only thing that had survived more or less intact. The webbing that had held her in place still dangled uselessly and all her instruments were fried or had been pried out, either by Felin's men or Thane's.

Not that it mattered—only the transport device had emergency battery power and that wouldn't last forever. Besides, the device needed the transport button to work.

She slid her hand to the protected pocket of the bulkhead where pilots stashed their most emergency of emergency devices. No scout left without an extra ration of food, hydrogenating crystals that would break down almost anything into drinking water and, most of all, the tiny, button-sized device that would broadcast his or her whereabouts to a fellow scout.

Lea palmed the button as Thane and Deon both hunkered down to peer inside the cockpit.

"'Tis strange magic," Deon said, running his fingers over metal plating. He touched the shaft that had thrust up between her knees. "What does this do?"

"Nothing now. But it was for steering."

"What pulled this vessel?" Deon's dark gaze roved the remaining dials in fascination. "You steer a cart with a yoke like this or a boat with a rudder. But you had no water to float on nor beast to pull you."

"Not pull, push," Lea said. "Boosted by rockets fed by fuel packs. All of which are dead, of course."

"*Fuelpacs,*" Deon repeated and glanced at Thane. "What kind of animal is a *fuelpac?*"

Lea tried not to laugh. "Not animal. Machine."

Thane had followed this discussion in silence, his dark eyes enigmatic. Now he spoke in a low voice. "You know it is not of Pamaar. This vessel came from beyond the Warding."

"What's the Warding?" Lea asked.

"It is the boundary that keeps us safe," Thane answered, though Deon shot him a warning glance. "The barrier between us and outer darkness. You should not have been able to get through. You should have..." He made a gesture with his arm.

"Bounced off?" Lea finished.

Was he talking about a force field of some kind? One that not only should have shunted her ship aside but one that kept this world from showing up on charts?

"If I'd bounced off, I'd have been toast. I would have run out of air, or one of the fine boys from the Four-One-Six would have made me a fireball just for fun."

Thane frowned. "You are saying these people wanted to kill you?"

"Wanted to, would love to, are dying to. I'm from the Rock. They want to harvest us and we don't want to surrender to them, so we're trying to figure out how to defend ourselves. Looks like you already found a way."

"Harvest?" Deon growled. "What do you mean *harvest*?"

Lea stood up and gazed at the valley, the cool breeze stirring her hair. "All this, dug out for the minerals. The city razed and anything valuable taken. They steal everything — water, materials, stone, even dirt if it's rich enough in carbon or fossils. All the people taken away and *recolonized* as they call it, though it's not much more than homeless shelters and indentured servitude. That's the Four-One-Six Quad Empire's modus operandi. They come, they see, they take what they want."

"You mean they're raiders," Deon grunted. "Like the northmen from the tiger-vessel clan."

"Raiders on a grand scale," Lea said. "They pretend to be oh-so civilized about it. Pack everyone off before they start harvesting, saying people from a backward planet need a better life."

"The darkness from outside the Warding," Thane said slowly. "When the Warding fails, we will face total destruction. That's what the legends say."

"Well, if they mean the Four-One-Six Empire, they're right. But this planet doesn't show up on any chart or readout — I only found it by accident. Whatever this Warding is, it's keeping you safe. The Rock isn't so lucky, which is why I have to get back there."

Thane watched her a moment, absorbing her words. Then suddenly he grabbed her wrist and twisted it, incredible strength opening her hand. He pried the tight-beam communicator from it and held it up between his fingers.

Lea tried to lunge for it, but Deon caught her in a viselike grip and locked one arm around her from behind.

Thane held the tiny communicator delicately. "What is this and what does it do?"

"Where did she get it?" Deon asked, tone frustrated.

"She took it from her ship."

"Shit. I never saw her do it."

"What is it?" Thane asked again.

Lea stopped struggling, realizing that Deon was damn strong and not about to let her go. "A tight-beam communication device. You're too late—I already used it."

Chapter Five
The Warding

☙

Deon watched Thane's eyes narrow, his slow anger building like a storm. Anyone who assumed Deon the strongest of the pair was wrong—where Deon was volatile, Thane had a cold strength that could make his enemies gibber in terror.

Lea wasn't exactly gibbering. She'd raised her chin and looked at Thane defiantly, though Deon felt her shaking.

"What did you do?" Thane asked in a deceptively calm voice. The wind stirred his white-blond hair, the red beads woven into it clicking softly.

"It sent a signal back to my people. *Only* my people, do you understand? It's coded and tight-beamed so that no one will trace it but my partner, Justin. He'll come and retrieve me and you can go back to enjoying your courtesans."

"Like a focus-stone," Deon said. Seers claimed they could communicate with each other by peering into stones, though he still thought seers were lunatics. "Except this one's from beyond the Warding."

Thane flicked his gaze back to Lea and his eyes took on a look of sorrow. That was another reason for Thane's strength—his compassion. He did what needed to be done, but he was never merciless.

"I'm sorry, Lea," Thane said. He picked up a hand-sized, flat rock and laid the device on another rock.

Lea struggled against Deon's grip. "No, please, I need that."

Thane gave her another sad look, but he was firm. "You are of Pamaar now."

He lifted the stone in his hand and smashed the device flat. Lea swore and fought, but Deon didn't let her go until Thane indicated for him to do so.

Lea raced to the rock and scooped up the smashed bits of metal. She stared down at them, head bowed.

"I can't let more people in through the Warding, Lea. It is dangerous enough that you came. If the Warding fails, we have nothing to protect us from the darkness."

She lifted her head, her face wet. "My people do not even have that. You at least have a shield."

"My people are already dying. We have not been penetrated by this harvesting empire you speak of, and yet the Wards are failing and people are dying. I should have all the power to save them, but I can do nothing."

Deon drew a sharp breath, not liking to see Thane so bleak, but this was the first time Thane had spoken of it out loud to anyone. Even to Deon, Thane didn't like to talk about the truth.

"The maid told me about your wife," Lea said. "Did she die because of these failing Wards?"

Thane never spoke about Cerena either. Deon assumed he'd shut out Lea's question, that he'd rise and walk away or snap at her to leave it alone.

Thane went down on one knee beside Lea and brushed back a strand of her variegated hair. "She grew very ill and it was the first time in my life that my healing powers failed. I tried everything I could think of, but she was beyond my skill. Others have been sickening and dying as well. Felin's clan, the falcon-sword clan, has been the most affected, and he hates me for it."

Hate was an understatement. Felin had threatened to overthrow Thane and to outright murder him. Never mind that the beautiful Cerena had died after going to Felin's clan to

65

try to help his people. She'd caught the same sickness and wasted away.

Lea's face softened and she put her hand on Thane's shoulder. "I'm so sorry."

"The sickness has not gone away and my ability to heal is waning."

"You healed *me* just fine."

"Injuries like yours—broken bones and such hurts—I am still able to handle. But this sickness…I can't reach it."

"My people have medicine against almost everything," Lea said. "If you let me get through to them, they can bring something to help."

Thane's expression turned weary. "The Warding can't slip any more than it already has and the king must heal his people. That is why he is allowed to continue being king."

Lea gave him a thoughtful look. "Legends from long, long ago on ancient Earth claimed that the touch of a king could heal. It was mostly BS and good propaganda, but you really can heal. I mean, you healed me just by touching me. What more do your people want?"

"No unexpected death and no disease."

"Oh is that all?"

He gave her a wry smile. "That is all."

"But that's way too much to expect of anyone. Even the best doctors can't heal everyone, even with kick-ass medical technology."

"Yes they *can* expect it. I am king of Pamaar, head of the lion-star clan. If I cannot keep the land and its people whole, I do not deserve to be king."

Lea fell silent, but Deon privately agreed with her. The lion-star clan expected Thane to be godlike and solve all their problems and the moment Thane couldn't help them, they turned against him. It pissed Deon off because Thane truly cared, and the fact that he couldn't be godlike for his people kept him awake all hours of the night.

Thane brushed Lea's hand with his again, the touch a caress. Deon narrowed his eyes as he watched. Thane hadn't shown much interest in any woman other than for necessary release since Cerena's death.

But Lea seemed to stir something to life in him, some spark that had been absent a while. Deon determined then and there that he'd nurture that spark to bring Thane back to his old self. He'd lock Lea in the palace and keep her there forever if that's what it took.

* * * * *

Thane was quiet on their ride back, Deon tight-lipped. Once they returned to the palace, the two men left Lea in her room, Thane saying he needed to take care of things—he would not say what things. There was no more mention of resuming the sexual play they'd started before the journey.

"I supposed he has to run the kingdom sometime," she said to herself as she strolled down an arched gallery, open to an airy hall below. Sunlight danced through stained glass skylights on the ceiling, flooding her with crimson, blue and gold.

The servants had let her leave Thane's private rooms without fuss and no guards followed her—at least not obviously. But she knew that if she tried to leave the palace or retrieve the things Thane had taken from her, she'd be stopped.

She'd been able to send the message at least, but only one, and who knew if Justin would receive it?

Scouts went on every mission knowing there was a real possibility they'd never come back. Usually they had little in their lives outside the corps—Lea had lost her family years ago, before she'd entered flight school. But that didn't mean she wanted to give up her entire life, her home, her friends, her mission, to stay here.

Thane was gorgeous, and when he did smile it was like sunshine warming a cold day. He was a strong man who could be caring at the same time—he put himself in pain to heal others. A person could bask in the warmth of that caring.

If only she'd come to this place for a little fun and R&R, *then* she'd gladly stay and see what interesting things Thane wanted to do. Not that this place would exist if it were easy to find for R&R. The Four-One-Six Empire didn't believe in letting anyone have fun.

She thought of Thane's body stretched over hers on the big bed and smothered a groan. With Thane it would be so *much* fun.

"Can I help you at all, my lady?" One of Thane's polite manservants had padded toward her at the sound of her groan. He was older and white-haired, wrapped in a toga-like garment, his pentacle tattoos standing out darkly on his pale skin.

"Am I right in thinking you don't have computers?" she asked him, trying to banish the memory of Thane's oh-so thorough kiss. When the man looked blank, she sighed. "No, of course you don't. I want to look something up, research something. How do I do that?"

"In the library, my lady. The Lord Thane has more books than any other person in the kingdom. It is this way."

Books. Of course. She'd never actually seen a book outside of pictures. Her curiosity mounting, she followed the man around the gallery and through a set of carved double doors into the strangest room she'd ever seen.

Shelves lined the oval room from floor to ceiling, crammed full of books. Lea stared in awe at the rich abundance. Back home, a book was a rare thing, so valuable they were in locked cases and guarded by motion sensors.

Thane's books were openly displayed, unprotected. She let her finger brush the spine of one and found it smooth, worn with age as though people actually *read* it.

"The index to the collection is there." The servant pointed to a large tome that stood open on a lectern near a massive table. "The numbers listed in it refer to which section and shelf you will find the books on each subject. This is section one." He pointed to the floor-to-ceiling shelf near the door. "If you require assistance, I can send for the cataloger."

"No, I just want to look. Um, thanks."

The servant bowed—another thing Lea wasn't used to. He pointed out the bell to summon him or another servant, then he departed on soft feet.

Lea moved to the index with uncertainty, but after flipping through a few pages of it, she caught onto the system, which was beautifully simple. She was used to looking up any required information in databases—you put in your search term and the engine revealed every piece of info from every database on the Rock, whether it was a printed file, an audio file or a stream of information that could be downloaded directly into your brain.

Here she had to look up words alphabetically, then walk to the shelf listed and locate the book, then find the information within the book. Once she lost her amazement of actually opening the book and turning the paper pages, her task grew easier.

What information she found on the Warding, however, was sketchy. Many legends had been woven around it, but the descriptions, while poetic, didn't much tell her what the Warding *was*.

Basically she learned that in the beginning was chaos and much death beyond the Warding. The ancestors of the four clans—lion-star, tiger-vessel, dragon-wand and falcon-sword—then arrived on Pamaar.

One of the leaders found the Warding and bound himself with it, and from then on, no chaos or war from beyond touched Pamaar. The ancestors destroyed the ancient vessels in which they'd arrived and settled down to farm the rich land.

Lea touched the page she read thoughtfully. It had been illustrated with colorful pictures scrolling down the margins of the first king surrounded by a glow, and people bent over hoes and plows with cheerful expressions on their faces.

Perhaps the chaos beyond the Warding had been a galactic war of some kind, the ancestors landing on Pamaar in escape pods from a destroyed ship. Perhaps the clans had been named after symbols on each pod—in large interstellar ships these days, passengers and crew were assigned to specific escape pods upon boarding. That way, if the ship had to be evacuated, you knew you went to escape pod blue-six on level ten, which eliminated a lot of panic and chaos.

Perhaps those ancient Pamaarans, if they were anywhere near as artistic as their descendents, had labeled their escape pods with animals and colorful symbols of the Tarot.

But this was fanciful speculation. The book she held didn't tell her for certain.

"What are you doing?"

Deon's fists came to rest on the table next to her, large, sinewy hands scarred from fighting. He'd changed into a coat and leggings of softer leather, his blue beads bright against his jet-black hair.

The man could move like a ghost. She'd never heard the door open or him cross the room, and she called herself a scout.

"Research," Lea said, keeping her voice steady.

He drew one of the open books to him and scanned the page. "The Warding. Why do you want to know so much about it?"

"I'm curious."

Deon rested one hip on the table and scowled at her. "If you think you can take it down so you can get away, you are wrong."

"I know I can't get away. You saw my ship—it's a burned-out wreck, *fucked up beyond all repair*, as we scouts like to say. And I'm willing to bet you don't have anything here that even flies in the stratosphere, even your drakes."

"Stratosphere? This is another of your words I don't understand."

"There are a whole slew of *your* words I don't understand. What is this Warding? These books aren't much help." She shoved one she'd been perusing away, impatient with it. "Is it magic? Because I don't believe in magic."

"What do you believe in?" Deon's dark eyes rested on her as though her answer were very important.

"My eyes, my hands, my experience and the fact that every meal in the pilot's mess will taste like sand mixed with bird crap."

He threw back his head and laughed, the rich sound ringing to the ceiling. "We had the same food at training camp. I am a soldier too, Lea, and I don't believe in magic either."

Lea had begun to smile with him, but she sobered. "Then what is hurting Thane?"

"I don't know." He looked troubled. He glanced down a moment, but she saw the flash of pain in his eyes before he hid it.

"Tell me about this Warding thing."

Deon looked up, his face clouded, but his gaze filled with anger and determination. "I will do better. I will show it to you."

She hid her sudden excitement by flinching. "Does this mean we have to fly on those drake things?"

He laughed again. "You fell from the sky in a ball of metal. Why are you afraid of drakes, who will never let you fall?"

"They have teeth."

Deon grinned and clapped her on the shoulder, the strength of him nearly shoving her over. "When they bite you, bite them back. They'll learn respect."

Somehow that didn't make Lea feel any better.

* * * * *

The Warding lay a hundred miles from the city, in the opposite direction from the crash site. The sun was setting when they reached it, the razor-sharp mountains on the horizon streaked purple and gold and blue.

Deon landed them in a field of sparse vegetation. The floor of this valley was desert sand, with only a few dry grasses and thorny bushes growing here, although those were studded with bright yellow flowers.

Deon unsaddled the drake and gave the animal a curt instruction Lea didn't understand. In some trepidation she watched the lizard-like beast hurtle itself into the air and flap away.

"You know he's our only way out of here," she pointed out. "I didn't see any towns or settlements for oh, a day's walk I'd say."

"He'll be back when he's eaten. You don't want a hungry drake around—they're cranky as hell."

He didn't seem in the least worried, so Lea decided not to worry either, or at least not to think about it. Deon had brought water for them and a little food, though not as much as she'd have packed for a desert expedition.

"So where is this Warding?" she asked.

"You're standing on it."

Lea looked down in amazement but saw only the desert floor. "I guess I expected something a little more dramatic."

"It's buried in the earth, has become part of it. There are caves over there that lead far underground. Come on."

He began hiking across the valley toward the base of the mountains, Lea following closely. The air was cool if dry, perfectly comfortable and even beautiful. It was only a few minutes walk to a crevice in the rocky hill that led to a dark cave.

Inside, Deon lifted candles from a shelf, blew the dust off them and lit them with a flint and stone and bit of wicking.

Lea took the lit candle he handed her. "You know, if you and Thane hadn't taken all my stuff, I would have had a much better light for us."

"Wouldn't have worked. The Warding likes only natural things and whatever you brought with you definitely isn't natural."

"Two candles aren't much against a huge cave."

"They don't need to last long. You will see."

He led her down a sloping tunnel that would have been wide and high enough for the drake to traverse. Lea knew she was trusting him with her life — he could kill her in the dark or simply abandon her. But she'd seen that flash of true caring in his eyes when they discussed Thane and knew he'd keep her alive as long as he thought she could help.

Lea watched his broad back in the flickering light as they moved along, his muscles playing under the leather — muscles she'd seen naked and strong. He and Thane were both beautiful men and any other scout would bless her luck being saved by two gorgeous males who had such an easygoing outlook about sex.

But though Thane hadn't put her in chains, she was still his prisoner. Deon had likely sent his drake off so she wouldn't try to use it to get away from him, not that she thought she had a chance of catching and riding the thing. For now she needed to bide her time and see what happened.

"Here."

Deon stopped and stepped back from a narrow opening in the tunnel. Lea looked past him and gasped.

A cavern opened at their feet, filled with shining, glowing light. Golden and magenta and blue and red light shimmered and glistened on the walls, the floor, the ceiling, radiant and beautiful. Deon was right—the candles were superfluous because the crystals beamed a rainbow so bright that her candle flame was a pale flicker against it.

"What is it?" There was no sound, yet at the same time Lea felt a vibration inside her as though the stones were singing—a song just for her.

"The Warding." Deon's voice was rich and low, the man as awed by the sight as she. "It is the heart of Pamaar, what guides us and keeps us safe."

"It's beautiful."

He gave her a look of approval. "It likes you too."

"How do you know that?"

"Legend has it that the Warding rejects any who try to bind with it but the true king. That's why not just anyone can issue the Challenge to the king."

"Well, I'm not trying to bind with it."

The lines around his eyes smoothed as though she'd passed some kind of test. "It's singing to you."

The vibrations echoed through her body until her heart and blood shimmered with it. She lifted her hand as though she could touch the light and swore she felt the tingle of it. She heard a slightly off note as well, as though one of the crystals was out of tune, but when she listened, she couldn't pinpoint it.

"Is that why you brought me here?" she asked Deon. "To see if I'd try to bind with it? To steal Thane's power?"

"Partly."

"And if I had tried?"

"The Warding wouldn't let you." His dark eyes glistened in the light of the crystals. "Even if it had, I'd have killed you."

"You really would, wouldn't you?" she asked without rancor. "Because you'd do anything to keep Thane safe."

"Is that so surprising? Thane is my life."

"Are you his?" Lea asked on sudden impulse.

Deon's eyes narrowed, but she read uncertainty in them. "You mean does he love me back? Of course he does—we're sacred-bonded. But he's king; do you know what I mean? Pamaar comes first. It has to."

"If he wasn't king, it could be just him and you," she pointed out. "If he doesn't get better and the people don't want him anymore, you and he could go off together. Be by yourselves."

"That shows you know nothing about Pamaar. If Thane can no longer be king, it is his duty to die. If no one Challenges him to a fight to the death, he should volunteer to kill himself."

Lea stared at Deon in shock. "Kill himself?"

"Yes," he answered grimly. "That's why I have to figure out what's going on and try to save him. Or I'll lose him forever."

"That is the most barbaric thing I've ever heard. The Pamaarans expect Thane to heal them and then when he can't, he has to die? Why?"

"So the new king can take over and heal the land again. The king and the land are one."

"That's ridiculous."

"Is it?" Deon asked fiercely. "Then why are Thane's healing powers fading and why are people dying? Felin's clan is the most affected and they're out for Thane's blood. They think it's long past time Thane did the decent thing and let

Felin Challenge him. To let him be slain so Felin can take over."

Lea looked past him at the singing, glowing crystals of the Warding. This must be the source of the shield that protected the planet; it must put off one hell of a power boost. Were the crystals the source of Thane's powers as well?

If the equipment in her ship hadn't fried, she could do a quick study on the Warding, figure out what it was radiating. As it was, she could only wonder and speculate.

"Neither of us believe in magic," she said slowly. "If this Warding thing is waning, then it won't give Felin any more power than it gives Thane. The falcon-sword clan might take over, but people will continue to die."

Deon's expression relaxed. "That's what I think too."

"What are we going to do?"

"We?"

Lea felt herself blush. "If I'm stuck here, I might as well help." She rolled her lip with her teeth. "If any of my equipment was in once piece, I might be able to figure all this out."

"You like Thane." It wasn't a question.

"You have to admit, he's compelling."

Deon's grin returned. "Compelling is one word for it."

"That doesn't mean... I mean, I'm not here to come between you."

Deon took a step toward her and she suddenly found herself against his formidable chest. His leather leggings couldn't disguise the very long cock that nudged her hip.

"Thane and I are bonded to one another, pledged in sacred ceremony." He brushed Lea's hair back from her forehead with blunt but gentle fingers. "When Thane falls in love, so do I. We always share."

"Like with Thane's wife?"

His eyes softened. "Cerena, yes. She was beautiful. Her death devastated Thane. And me."

"I'm sorry."

As weird as Lea thought two men loving and sharing the same woman was, Thane's grief was unmistakable and she sensed similar grief from Deon. And anyway, who was she to judge the customs of another people? They had sorrow and love and gladness and fear, just as people on the Rock did.

"I'm truly sorry," she repeated, her heart aching for him.

"I know you are." Deon pressed his lips to the line of her hair and his gruff voice softened. "That's why I didn't argue when Thane didn't want to lock you up. He sensed when he healed you that you'd understand." He paused. "Well, I didn't argue *much*."

"You don't trust me."

"I don't trust anyone. Not where Thane is concerned."

"I can't blame you." She reached up and did what she wouldn't have dared when she first met him, touched his hard face with her fingertips. "You know nothing about me. I could have been sent to destroy your Warding and kill your king. But I wasn't. I'm sorry about what's happening here and I'll try to help if I can."

"What a sweetheart."

His smile was warm, though his eyes still held wariness. Maybe it was the Warding and its compelling song, maybe it was Deon's obvious and intense love for Thane—whatever caused it, she followed her impulse and raised on her tiptoes to kiss his mouth.

Deon caught her with his hand at her nape, not letting her keep the kiss brief. He opened his mouth with his lips, the kiss hard and strong, what she'd expect from a warrior. He kissed her with a thoroughness of an experienced lover, one who knew what he wanted and exactly what she wanted.

Thane's kiss had aroused her and filled her with unbearable need. Deon's kiss promised a different kind of need—fiery, intense, maybe even brutal. But satisfying. So satisfying. She remembered how he looked in the bedroom, walking across the room stark naked, ready to obey Thane's commands.

He snaked his hand under her tunic, rough palm on her bare back. "The Warding has power, can you feel it?"

She nodded. Standing in the glow of light made the last of her soreness fade and revived her energy.

"I want Thane," she whispered. She hadn't meant to say it out loud, but the Warding seemed to drag truth out of her. It also heightened her senses and her desire.

"So do I," Deon murmured. He skimmed his callused hand to her breast and gently plucked at her nipple.

Two days ago her soaring response would have alarmed her. Now she gladly let her quim pool and her blood warm, and the constant singing of the Warding threw her inhibitions to the wind. Deon was tall and powerful and dangerous, and she wanted to wrap herself around him.

How is it that I wouldn't mind having both of them? The scout sex ed classes never covered this.

Deon nuzzled her cheek. "Take your pants off."

"Gee, you really know how to sweet-talk a girl."

He put his lips close to her ear, breath hot. "Take them off or I'll rip them off."

She understood it wasn't an idle threat. With shaking fingers she unclasped the fly, then toed off her boots and shoved her leggings down. She pulled off the tunic as well, liking how the close air of the cave hugged her skin.

He looked her up and down, taking his time, and she stood back and let him. She shifted her feet apart and did what he wanted her to do back in the bedroom, dipping her fingers to her quim.

Deon let his gaze linger there until she thought she could feel his stare pressing her clit. Then he grinned and turned away to strip off un-self-consciously. He was a fighter and an athlete, his body taut with muscle, his broad shoulders rippling.

The lion tattoo on his arm moved with his bicep, the tattoo on his pelvis tight and firm. But for all his strength, when he lifted her against his body, he was gentle.

"How do you like it?" he asked.

"Um — the normal way. I guess."

His low laughter wrapped her like a blanket. "I see you need teaching, love."

She grasped a beaded braid that hung beside his face. "I like Thane's way."

Deon nodded, his eyes darkening as he lowered his head to nip her neck. "I like his way too. Hold on tight."

Chapter Six
Knowledge

Deon knew he'd never be able to take her calmly. The Warding rang through his body and she was a sweet armful, this woman from beyond the barrier with her strange green eyes. Beautiful and dangerous.

She wrapped her bare legs around his hips as he lifted her, a half-smile playing on her mouth. Daring him, testing him, teasing him.

Her breasts were soft little globes against his chest, her ass firm and round against his palms. She was a soldier like he was, but she was all woman. His cock thickened and moved unerringly to her opening, finding it slick and wet and ready for him.

Nothing elaborate, he decided. Just him in her, finding out what she was made of.

He backed her against the cavern wall, shielding her with his arms so the rock wouldn't scrape her back. Her eyes were heavy, her touch on his face sweet.

Sweet. Deon liked it rough, which is what he'd liked about Cerena. She wanted it both gentle and hard, and she and Deon and Thane had fucked far into the night on many occasions.

In this place, it would be hot and raw and fierce. He let his cock part her pussy lips, teasing the sensitive folds until her eyes closed to jade slits. Her hum of delight made his cock throb, but he held back, wanting her to crave it.

He loved her tousled hair, cropped short like a soldier's but varying in colors from butter-yellow to golden-brown. Her skin was smooth and smelled musky and clean, beautiful even without tattoos.

"Gods, you're fine," he whispered, his voice breaking.

"You're pretty fine yourself, king's man."

"Do you want me all the way?" he asked, kissing her beautiful hair.

"*Yes.*"

"Are you sure?" He grinned. "You have to be really sure."

"Damn it, Deon, *fuck me.*"

"I don't know… "

She settled it by clutching his ass with her legs and shoving herself down onto his waiting cock.

She groaned at the same time he did—*oh fucking damn,* she was tight.

"Deon," she gasped.

"It's all right, love. You're taking me good."

Was she ever. Her sheath squeezed him like a glove, the slick, wet femaleness of her clenching him hard.

Her breath was warm on his face, her skin flushed. She might be a woman who fell to Pamaar in a burning star, but she was human, female, soft-skinned and soft-eyed. She was the best thing he could have—a woman would could fight at his side by day and fuck with him all night.

She tilted her head back against the rock wall, the Warding humming and singing with all its might. "Goddess, you're too big for me," she moaned.

"No, we fit just right," he said. He held her firmly and drove in another inch. "Like that?"

For answer she kissed him, her tongue snaking into his mouth in hot, wet jabs.

This was pure fucking, ripe and needy. They were both wound up by the Warding, she wet and slippery, his cock rock-hard. They were complete—almost.

Thane needed to be there, then it would be perfect. He'd lean against the rock wall beside them, maybe lace his arm around Deon's shoulders and kiss Lea. He'd slide his hand between them and touch where Deon and Lea joined, or maybe circle behind Deon and slip his cock between Deon's legs so that Deon could feel Thane's staff brush his balls.

Deon imagined the feel of Thane's cock rubbing his where it went into Lea, the heated friction plus the warmth of Thane's hard body against his back.

"Perfect," he whispered. "Perfect."

"What's perfect?"

"If Thane were here, touching us while we fucked."

"Oh—*yes.*" Lea's pussy began convulsing, wicked little throbs that squeezed his cock without mercy. He grunted as he shoved himself as far into her as he could, thrusting hard. His focus narrowed to nothing but this feeling and her fine green eyes.

When his imaginary Thane bit his ear and whispered *I love you,* he rocked his head back and released his seed deep inside her, his shout mixing with the mad singing of the Warding.

Lea continued twisting her sweet pussy on him while sweat coated his skin and his heart thudded like he'd just run ten miles nonstop. He held her close, his shaft still hard as she wound down from her own ecstasy. The Warding wound down with her, its frantic music easing to a shimmering hum.

After a while, Lea opened her eyes and gave him a tired smile. "Wow."

Deon didn't understand the word, but he caught its meaning. "Wow," he repeated.

Lea wrapped her arms around him and gave him a warm, sensuous kiss. She didn't have the practiced touch of a courtesan—she was simply a woman kissing a man she'd just made love with.

Not trying to beguile him—enjoying what they'd shared.

Dangerous. This woman was so, so dangerous.

"Is this why you brought me out here?" she murmured.

"Partly," he admitted. "It was part of the reason. I couldn't let Thane touch you until I was sure."

"Sure about what?"

"Whether you were safe."

She pulled back a little, looking at him in puzzlement. "What do you mean *safe?* You two took my only weapon and destroyed my communicator. I'm pretty damn safe."

"You might have been booby-trapped. Had a pussy full of poison or something."

She stared. "You're kidding me, right?"

"We know nothing about you or where you come from. You're an irresistible woman and who knows if you weren't sent to seduce and kill him?"

"Let me get this straight—you were willing to have sex with me even though I might have killed you, just to save Thane?"

"Yep."

"Wow." That word again. "That's noble, in a bizarre sort of way. But not necessary. I'm not crazy enough to booby-trap myself to kill someone with sex. I prefer a straight fight."

He let himself smile. "But it was fun finding out I was wrong."

She gave him a lazy kiss. "Of course you'd think that."

"Was it fun?"

"What do you think?"

He was spared having to answer by a thump and a blast of hot hair. Suddenly the cave was full of drake, bending his sinuous neck to put his head at Deon's level. Cutie's bright blue eyes blinked and he cocked his head.

"Welcome back, drake-breath," Deon said. "We'll be out in a minute."

Cutie gave him a look of what could only be pure disgust, but turned and waddled out of the cave, his wings pressed tight to his sides.

Deon carefully slid Lea to her feet and reached for his clothes. *"He's* ready to go home, so we should be too. Bloody beasts."

"Deon."

Lea had moved to the edge of the precipice overlooking the Warding.

"What?"

"Look just there."

He came to her and followed her pointing finger to the far corner of the cave, which was almost lost in shadow.

"Look at what?" he asked.

"I thought I heard it when we first came in. Like something out of tune." She stabbed her finger off to the right. "Do you see it?"

Deon shaded his eyes and peered into the light. At first all he saw were the crystals glowing and sparkling as usual. Then he discerned a slight dimness in the far corner and, as he looked, he could make out a black area, where crystals should be dancing in light and weren't.

As though his attention on them made it worse, the light of the entire Warding dampened slightly, allowing him to see a chunk of it dead or dying.

"I sure as hell don't like that."

"Is that what's wrong with it?" Lea asked.

Deon scanned the Warding a while longer, foreboding inside him. Thane knew the Warding had weakened, but to see it stark and black where it never had been before made his blood cold.

Lea put her hand on his arm, her eyes anxious, her touch attempting comfort. He drew her up to kiss her warm lips, then laced his arm around her waist and led her from the caves, both of them silent.

* * * * *

Lea was happy to see Thane's fairy-tale castle loom up in front of them and solid ground beneath her feet once more. She loved to fly, but in a *ship*, not perched on the back of a winged monster.

The drake gave her what could only be an evil grin as she slipped out of the saddle and hobbled back to the castle. Deon's grin was definitely evil and he slapped her on the rump as she passed.

She so needed a hot bath. With bubbles. Justin had always teased her about her girly affection for bubble baths and scented soap. She'd replied that she might be a scout with military training, but she was female underneath her unisex suit and liked to be feminine once in a while.

Deon had just proved that without a doubt.

Her face heated as she remembered…

She was given a long, leisurely meal with exquisite food and smooth, red wine. She ate alone, attended by five servants who hovered anxiously and watched her eat every bite.

Then the motherly maid who had tended her before settled her in a steaming tub and departed just as the courtesans Emilie and Balin came into the bath chamber. The pair wore little clothing—Balin in nothing but a loincloth and Emilie in a short, body-hugging silk tunic that left her arms and legs bare.

"Where is Thane?" Lea asked, up to the neck in bubbles. Happily, the castle had a profusion of bath salts, oils and foam, though it had been difficult narrowing her choice to one.

Emilie smiled. "In council with Lord Deon."

"Does that mean…?"

"No," Balin answered in his deep voice. "In council with his councilors. Lord Felin has been stirring up trouble again."

Lea sighed, thinking of the chilling darkness in the Warding. "I wish I could help. I wish I could do *something*." She slapped at the water, sending bubbles over Balin's bare chest as he leaned over her.

Balin gave her a sympathetic smile as he brushed the suds away. "It is difficult to watch someone you care for in trouble. He asked that we look after you. You can help him by enjoying your stay here so he does not worry about you."

"I can help him by letting courtesans have their way with me?"

Balin chuckled and Emilie's professional smile returned. "You do not have to have sex if you do not wish it. But we can bathe you and massage you and even sing to you if you like."

"Do all Thane's guests get the royal treatment?"

"Not at all." Emilie trailed her finger across Lea's shoulder. "Which makes me think you are very special to Thane."

Lea wasn't sure what to make of that. Balin slipped behind the tub and began kneading the muscles of her neck and, with a groan, she let him. If Thane wanted her pampered, who was she to refuse?

* * * * *

"You took her to the Warding?" Thane's throat went tight with anger as he faced Deon alone. The council meeting had lasted only an hour, but Thane had been impatient to return to his rooms with Deon and interrogate him.

Deon shrugged, trying to look innocent. "She wanted to know about it. I figured if I let her see the truth, she wouldn't try to sneak away from us to see for herself."

"Do you realize how dangerous that was?" Thane snapped. "Of course you did, and you went anyway."

"We needed to know," Deon said stubbornly.

"Whether or not she was deceiving us? If the Warding had struck out at her, it could have killed you too, you bloody idiot."

"It didn't."

Thane clenched his large fists. "You couldn't have known that. I *need* you, and not only because I love you. I need you beside me every step of the way and losing you would not have helped me just now. Did you think of that?"

Deon's face was a mask of obstinacy. "I knew you'd forbid it. But we know for sure now, don't we, that she hasn't been sent to try to destroy you. We had to find out."

"So you decided walking right up to the Warding was the best way? Have you lost your mind? Just because you were right doesn't mean it wasn't stupid."

"I know it was stupid. But so is keeping her around you without knowing whether Felin sent her to take you down, or if she really is a dark being from beyond the Warding."

"Which is why I have her watched every second. I want her to be on our side, but I'm not the gullible fool you think I am."

"You're falling for her," Deon said. "I see the way you look at her. You're picturing yourself presenting her to the kingdom as the next queen. You're measuring for a new bed and cradles for your children."

"I haven't gone as far as that. If you don't remember, I'm dying."

"Not if I can help it."

Thane growled. "Getting yourself killed won't exactly help, Deon. I don't want you leaving the castle without me, even if I have to chain you up in a dungeon."

"You don't have a dungeon."

"I'll *build* one."

Deon cleared his throat. "Sorry, Your Majesty."

Thane let it go. Deon rarely apologized and Thane knew his friend truly did realize how stupid he'd been. Lea's arrival had made them both edgy and neither was thinking straight.

"Where is she? Still in the bath?"

"Yes."

"Well, at least you're keeping track of her." He pulled off the silk robe he'd worn at the council meeting and tossed it aside. "Come with me. But only to stand guard. You deserve a little punishment."

Deon scowled, but not as much as he should have. In fact, he looked slightly smug.

"Don't tell me," Thane said.

"You know I had to make sure she was safe before I let her touch you."

Thane pinched the bridge of his nose. "You made love to her at the Warding."

"It's my duty as your personal guard to make sure anyone who comes to your bed isn't a danger."

That was true, but the smug look was getting irritating. "Yes, I'm sure it was a huge sacrifice on your part."

Deon grinned. "I love my job."

"Don't talk any more, Deon, or I really will build a dungeon." Thane put a heavy hand on his lover's leather-clad shoulder. "Just for you."

* * * * *

Lea opened her eyes to see Thane lowering himself into the bath with her. He settled on the opposite end of the huge tub, water and bubbles lapping his bare collarbone. His white-blond hair floated in the water, the red beads in it bright against the foam.

"May I bathe with you, Lea?"

His voice was low, formal, his eyes dark and shuttered. She sensed that the answer to the question was important.

"Of course," she answered. A moot point anyway, since he was already in the water with her.

Deon sat backward on a chair on the other side of the room, his legs splayed open, his huge frame dwarfing the delicate piece of furniture. He kept his clothes on and his expression grim.

Balin continued massaging Lea's neck and Emilie strummed the stringed instrument she'd brought out, humming a soothing tune.

"Emilie," Thane said, his eyes flicking to her. "It is your daughter's birthday."

"Indeed." She smiled warmly. "She is ten years old today. She is most grateful for the gift you sent."

"Go home and spend this special day with her. Give her my regards."

Emilie looked pleased. She wrapped the instrument in its velvet cloth and quietly gathering up her things. Thane remained silent until she'd pulled a robe over her tunic and left the room.

"Shall I stay?" Balin asked. His fingers had eased every knot from Lea's neck.

"If you like. Massage Deon. He's tense. I would like to speak to Lea alone."

Balin stood up, drying his fingers on the mountain of towels next to the bath, then he bowed and moved across the cavernous room to Deon. Thane waited until Balin and Deon had begun a low-voiced conversation, then he beckoned to Lea.

"Come to me."

Lea came from a culture in which a man never commanded a woman to do anything, not unless he wanted a punch in the mouth. But for some reason, Lea didn't mind—

because she wanted to do what he said, not because he forced her.

She left the seat at her end of the tub and floated to him. He caught her around the waist and eased her to his lap facing him.

"Deon took you to the Warding."

"He did." She tilted her head to study his dark eyes.

"It is forbidden for anyone but the king and ones bonded to him to look upon it."

"Really? Then why is the cave wide open? No signs saying *keep out if you're not the king or his best friend*?"

"Why should we need signs? Everyone knows it is forbidden. Deon is permitted to go, but he knew he should not have taken you."

Lea glanced across the room. "Is that why he's so pissed off?"

"He should not have done it, but in a way, it is good he did. It was a test and you passed."

"He implied that when we were there. That he'd kill me if I tried to bind with the Warding."

"There's more to it than that. Not everyone can stand being so close to the Warding. It might have killed you. If you were an enemy of Pamaar, a demon from the darkness, it would most definitely have killed you."

"Oh." A shiver went through her that the bathwater couldn't warm. "Terrific. Nice of him to tell me."

"He was wrong to do it and I have explained to him why." Thane's dark gaze fixed intently on her as he touched her cheek. "But in a way, I am glad. Because now I know you are not my enemy."

Lea didn't understand how he knew. She still could be an agent from the empire scouting for the best place to start harvesting. But she liked his fingers brushing her face and the feel of his strong body under hers, so she decided not to bring it up.

When he kissed her, she knew she was in the worst danger of her life. She was starting to care about Thane and Deon and their people, and she couldn't let herself. She was a scout with a mission to protect the Rock at all costs. If she were stranded or captured, it was her first duty to get away and report all she could to her phalanx leader.

She could not want to be with these men. But Thane, with sadness buried inside him and a touch like fire, was stealing her heart.

Justin would laugh himself sick.

Justin is not here, a little voice inside of her pointed out.

Thane's lips were warm and firm, jaw sandpaper rough under her touch. He tasted like spice and wine, smelled of the bathwater and male. She moved her hand to the cock that jutted between them and squeezed it. He was hard and heavy and when her hand contracted, he moaned in his throat.

Notwithstanding the incredible sex she'd had in the caves with Deon, she wanted Thane with breathtaking intensity. His cock was nice and thick under her fingers, the flange silken soft. She stroked back and forth with her thumb until he rested his forehead against hers, breath warm on her skin.

"I am imagining you with a tattoo here," he said, trailing his fingers down her neck. "A beautiful lion with amazing colors. It would become you."

"I can't possibly get a tattoo." She found it hard to speak.

"You must, if you are to be mine. A star here." He touched the skin below her ear. "And again on your back, just here." His fingers moved to the hollow at the base of her spine. "So that when I enter you, I can look down and know for certain you belong to me."

"Thane." Lea made herself meet his sin-dark gaze. "You're moving too fast for me."

"I must do so. You must be made of the lion-star clan before I present you to Pamaar. If you have no clan, then you will be considered from beyond the Warding, no matter that the Warding did not harm you."

Lea went still, not liking the grave look in his eyes. "Let me guess. If I'm not of a clan, I get killed."

He nodded. "It is the law. But I would never let that happen."

Lea fell silent. Thane was trying to protect her, she saw that, but she sensed a net slowly closing around her. If she became one of them, if she cared too much, she'd not want to leave. And she had to go.

"The best artist will be brought for you," Thane went on. "Your tattoos will be the most exquisite in the clan."

Lea held up dripping hands. "Just stop. You've brought me the best food, the best courtesans, the best wine and you'll bring me the best tattoo artist. But you're leaving out the one thing I want most—to go home."

Her voice wavered over the word. Home—the Rock, with its windstorms that drove everyone to seek shelter underground, the gagging smell of sulfur fields far to the south, the camaraderie in the barracks, waking to the smell of thick coffee in the mornings.

Thane's world was beautiful and exotic and Thane treated her like a princess. But the longing to see the stark harshness of her home, remembering the sound of her father's laughter over the lowing of the stubborn livestock on the simple farm where she'd grown up suddenly overwhelmed her. The Rock was so far away and here she was, trapped in this lavish kingdom, alone.

Tears spilled out of her eyes to drip into the heated water, breaking the bubbles. She put her hands to her face to stop them, but they seeped around her fingers.

She felt Thane's strong arms close around her and pull her close. She leaned against his shoulder, giving up trying to stem the tears.

Deon moved from his perch across the room, but Thane held up his hand, stilling him.

"You belong to me now," he whispered to her, lips brushing her hair. "I will take care of you."

She wanted to argue, but she was so damn tired from the long flight with Deon to the Warding and back, not to mention the rough and fast sex. Plus her mind was weary with all she had to absorb and trying to stave off the knowledge that she could very well be stuck here for life.

Pamaar was a beautiful place, but dangerous. She knew full well that without Thane's protection, she'd be screwed.

It was easier not to think about it. Much better to lay here and soak up the warmth of the bath and Thane and the steam of the room.

Thane could have locked her up or tortured her or outright killed her when Deon first brought her in. Instead he acted like he cared, which twisted a knife in her heart. Even gruff-voiced Deon had made sure she wasn't hurt at the Warding and had held her steadily on the drake.

If they were going to capture her and keep her, why did they have to be so *nice* about it?

And why did Thane have to be so gorgeous and compassionate and brokenhearted?

"You did this on purpose," she mumbled.

Thane bent to catch her words. "Did what on purpose?"

"Made yourself irresistible."

He sent her his heart-melting smile. "Do you find me irresistible? I'm glad. I find you highly desirable."

"So much talking," Deon said, hulking next to the bath. "Are you going to fuck or what?"

* * * * *

"Thank you, you have been helpful."

Felin lounged back in his camp chair and regarded his informer, who stood outlined in flickering firelight—someone so close to Thane Felin couldn't help but feel glee.

"So the seers vow that the queen has returned with the falling star, but King Thane is no better and people are still dying. Interesting."

He spoke calmly, but anger roiled through him. Thane was a liar, and he should have long since faced the Challenge or fallen on his sword and spared them all. When Felin became king, he'd find a way to save his people. If he had to capture the "queen" and make use of her, so be it.

He snapped his fingers. His second came to him with a velvet pouch, which he opened to reveal a brooch, an intricate dragonfly encrusted with diamonds and other precious stones.

"A gift for your daughter," he said. "I believe it is her birthday today?"

"It is," Emilie said, accepting the brooch. "It is kind of you to remember."

Felin merely smiled. Emilie had been easy to bribe, because her daughter had fallen ill and Thane's powers were as nothing to save her. Felin had promised that if Emilie helped him, her daughter would be the first restored when Felin became king. Emilie hadn't hesitated long.

Felin dismissed his second and the servants and his tent rapidly emptied, leaving Emilie and himself alone. He hooked his finger through Emilie's silk belt and pulled her down to his lap.

"Thank you," he said again. "I don't know what I'd do without you."

"Of course." Emilie smiled at him, the beautiful, practiced courtesan's smile.

She ran her hands down his torso and loosened his leggings, then slid to her knees and, still smiling, began to pleasure him in her perfect, courtesan way.

Chapter Seven
Betrayal

೫

Deon had a good point, Thane thought. Thane was hard and ready and Deon was bulging out of his leggings again. Lea was a sweet, bare armful. She might be a soldier, but she was scared and vulnerable and Thane felt incredibly protective of her.

As angry as Thane was at Deon, he was grateful to his friend for finding out truths, though he didn't like Deon's methods. But he wasn't going to let Deon off easy. The punishment he had in mind made his cock sway.

"I might be king of Pamaar," he murmured, kissing Lea's hair. "But in this room, I am your slave. My only pleasure will be giving you pleasure."

Her eyes widened, those beautiful jade-colored eyes, so strange yet already precious to him. "Don't tempt me like that," she said.

"What gives you pleasure, Lea? Would you like Balin to take you? He is highly trained."

Lea's glance darted to Balin who sat with one arm over his knee, looking as sensuous as ever. Thane felt her pulse quicken and knew she found the idea exciting.

"No," she stammered. "I mean, I'm not trying to be rude, but I don't think I'm quite comfortable with the whole courtesan thing."

"In this room, at this time, your desires are all that matters. Balin understands." He ran light fingers across her skin and enjoyed feeling her shiver. "You have already sampled the delights of Deon. Would you like that again?"

She turned ruby red. "He told you about that? Figures."

"He was doing his job, protecting me."

Deon chuckled. "I live for my work."

"Or would you like me to pleasure you slowly?" Thane asked, watching her reactions carefully. "Would you like me to please you with my tongue? Or my fingers?"

He slid his hand under the water and brushed the button of her clit. She jumped most satisfactorily.

"You like that," he said.

She clutched him. "Just take me and get it over with. I'm about to explode."

Thane smiled, his cock more rigid by the second. "We will go slow. I'm very big—you need to get used to me."

"You don't need to lock me in a dungeon and torture me. You're doing it right now."

"Torture?" Thane said in mock surprise. He slid one finger into her quim, finding hot sleekness the water couldn't wash away. "This is torture?"

She moved against his hand. "You know it is."

"You want me," he said. "Good."

"Of course I want you." She gasped as his second finger slid inside. "I've wanted you since you put your hands on me and healed me. That felt so damn *good.*"

"Healing is supposed to feel good," he said in some surprise.

"Orgasmic good?"

"Why not?"

She growled. "No wonder everyone wants you to heal them."

"Right now, I want to pleasure you. Stand up."

Lea ground herself against his fingers. "I don't want to. I thought you were the slave here."

"It will feel even better, love. Stand for me."

Allyson James

She slid—slowly and reluctantly—away from him, moaning again when his fingers came out of her. She stood up in the bath, water and bubbles cascading from her slim body.

She was tightly muscled all over, but her breasts hung in round globes, the tips pointed and dark. The hair at her quim was a twist of wiry golden softness. Deon's eyes became pools of black as he looked her over, the tip his cock parting the laces of his leggings.

Thane pressed her legs open with his palms and leaned to tease her clit with his tongue.

"Ohh," she purred. "Torture."

"For all of us," Deon said.

Thane raised his head. "You know why you're not in here with me."

"Punishment, yeah. I think I've learned my lesson."

"Not even close."

"Come on, Thane, she's not the only one who's going to explode."

"You have no self-control, my friend. Very well, join us." He grinned. "I'll punish you later."

"Thought you'd never ask."

Deon shucked his clothes and surged into the water behind Lea, his entrance sloshing bubbles and water over the sides. He snaked his arms around her, brown hands resting on her pale abdomen, his big thighs pressing the backs of hers.

Thane went back to licking her. Sweet honey. She was beautiful and tasted like the finest wine—better. He'd never had anything so exquisite in his mouth.

The longing in her voice when she'd said she wanted to go home had caught in his heart. He had no ability to send her back and that angered him, as much as he wanted her to stay. When he died, Deon would protect her, but that thought wouldn't make leaving her easier.

I will not let them win. I will not let it win. I have something to live for — this beautiful woman. I can't abandon her after the gods brought her here.

He laughed inside himself. *And I can't let Deon have all the fun.*

Lea writhed under his ministrations, the sounds coming from her throat enchanting. Deon had his hands on Lea's breasts, his mouth on her neck. Thane reached around Lea and pressed his fingers into Deon's taut buttocks, and Deon shifted in pleasure.

This was heaven, his mouth over Lea's hot, tight clit, his hands on Deon's ass. He dipped his finger between Deon's cheeks, letting the tip find the anal star and gently press in. Deon responded by groaning out loud and sucking Lea's neck.

It was like a dance — Thane rubbed his tongue all over Lea's clit and played with Deon's anal star, Deon thrust his cock between Lea's thighs and rolled her nipple between his fingers, she leaned against Deon and arched her pussy at Thane. The three of them rocked simultaneously in pleasure, three times as good as sex with only two.

When Lea came, it was beautiful. Honey poured into Thane's mouth and he lapped it up, running his tongue inside her pussy to get every drop. She pushed herself against his mouth, her cries muffled as Deon caught them on his lips.

Primal joy slashed through him. He loved Deon and it had been a long time since they'd pleasured a woman together. They played with the courtesans, but it had been years since they'd concentrated their efforts to bring a woman to as much ecstasy as they possibly could.

He looked up. Lea rested her head on Deon's shoulder, her eyes closed, while Deon nibbled her neck. His thin black braids touched the water, the ends of his hair curling.

"You like to dance, Lea," Thane said. "You please me."

"She's beautiful," Deon murmured, fingers splayed across her breasts.

Lea opened her eyes and glanced across the room, but Thane knew before he looked that Balin had gone. The male courtesan was discreet and had an uncanny knack for knowing what his clients wanted—even when it was for him to be elsewhere. Balin knew that Lea was shy with the courtesans, so he'd beat a retreat. Maybe later, Thane could show her how not to be shy.

"I'd like to pleasure *you*, now," she said.

Thane shook his head. "This is all about you. I'm not finished."

"I thought you were supposed to be my slave. It pleases me to put my mouth on you."

Deon chuckled. "You have to learn, Lea, my love. He says he's a slave but he's still the king, so he makes the rules. He doesn't really understand how to play this game."

Thane knew damn well what he was doing, but he allowed Deon his joke. He rose to his feet, water cascading, and lifted Lea in his arms. Her body was wet and slippery and lush, a joy to hold as he climbed out of the bath and took her into her bedroom.

Deon followed with towels.

Once Lea lay naked on a nest of towels, Thane showed her everything he knew about pleasure. He used his tongue and his hands all over her body, then Deon joined him and they licked her to climax again. Thane brought out toys, soft and hard, and he and Deon played with her.

She screamed climax again and again, until she fell back, exhausted, her multi-colored hair curling on her damp forehead. She whimpered.

"If I don't have you inside me, I'm going to die."

"But if I make you wait, it will be all the sweeter," Thane whispered in her ear. He let his hardened cock brush her quim and she cursed in frustration. He didn't tell her that he was dying for her too, that it took every ounce of willpower not to spread her wide and fuck her hard, *now*.

"I need you," she moaned.

Thane stretched himself full-length beside her, his lips at her ear. "You've already had Deon."

"Not the same."

"Oh thanks," Deon growled.

"I mean — it was different."

"Thanks, again. I guess we can't all be king."

"It has nothing to do with him being a king." Lea half sat up in frustration. "I just want *him.*"

"Shh," Thane soothed her. "Go to sleep now."

Lea flopped down, her cheeks flushed and eyes heavy. "I'll make you pay for this, just you wait."

Thane laughed softly. "I'm looking forward to it." He touched her brow, sending his healing magic to her — what little he could do these days. "Sleep now."

She closed her eyes, limbs slack, and took a long breath. "Thank you," she whispered.

Thane kissed her lips until her breathing grew slow and steady, then he reluctantly lifted himself away.

✳ ✳ ✳ ✳ ✳

Lea didn't completely go to sleep. She drowsed for a time, eyes closed, and listened to the two men who had just shown her more ecstasy than she'd known existed.

"Sure, work us up and then put her to sleep," Deon said, his voice low. "Where are courtesans when you need them?"

"I'm still here," Thane said.

There was a long silence.

"Don't start this again," Deon rumbled.

"I don't know how much longer I can hang on," Thane replied. He sounded weary. "And I've never had you."

"We follow the rules. It sucks, but if anyone has a hint that the king doesn't obey his own laws, even this one, they'll be on you even faster. They'll use any excuse to kill you."

"A law that says I can't treat the man I love, who is more loyal to me than any other, as an equal is a bad law."

"Hey, you're the king—I'm a soldier. Deal with it. And don't think I haven't had fantasies about me fucking you until you can't walk for three days. I have that fantasy every day."

Lea felt the bed move as Thane moved behind Deon. "In this fantasy, are *you* unable to walk for three days?"

"Yes. But I find things to do with my time. Like fucking you some more."

"Good fantasy."

Deon laughed softly. "I think so."

Thane's humor died. "I need you."

"About time you admitted that."

The bed moved some more. Lea forced her eyes open to slits, too interested to succumb to sleep. She saw Deon position his large body on all fours, weight resting on his forearms. Thane loomed behind him, his cock huge and swollen, his fingers covered with lube from the bedside table.

Thane's hand moved on Deon's ass and then he braced himself on Deon's hips and slid inside him.

Deon's eyes squeezed shut. "Oh holy…"

"Shh. Don't wake Lea."

Deon bit his bottom lip, but he couldn't help grunting and groaning in his throat. Behind him, Thane began to rock his hips, only a little, fingers on Deon's flesh, eyes narrowed in concentration.

They made love in near silence, two beautiful men so close to Lea in the bed, locked together, swaying a bit as Thane pumped into Deon. Deon curled his fingers around the pillow, his face twisted as he tried to contain his pleasure.

"Do you like me fucking you?" Thane asked, his voice soft but almost savage.

"You know I do. Damn you."

"Don't wake Lea," he repeated.

Deon looked over his shoulder. "You're a bastard."

Thane grinned. "You love it."

"Sure, right... Oh fucking damn, I'm going to come..."

"No." Thane gripped Deon's hips harder. "Not until I'm ready."

Deon let out a string of whispered expletives but held himself in, the chords on his neck standing out.

"Almost there," Thane whispered. "Not yet."

"Fuck you."

"No, I'm fucking *you*. This is what happens when you disobey me."

More expletives. Deon's face was red, his fingers tearing rents in the sheets.

"Now!" Thane threw his head back, his hips moving faster and faster, a look of bliss on his face. "Oh yes, gods, now. You're fucking sweet."

Deon muffled his roar in the pillows and came all over the towels still spread on the bed. Thane rode him a little longer, both of them taking a while to finish.

Finally Thane withdrew and Deon crashed onto his side next to Lea. Thane stood beside the bed, looking down at his lover, his cock still slick and hard, then he leaned over and pressed a kiss to Deon's back.

"Thank you," he murmured and Lea finally slid into a deep, erotic, dream-filled sleep.

When she awoke, it was daylight. Deon snored next to her under the sheets, the towels gone, his arm curled under his head. Of Thane, there was no sign.

Lea stirred and yawned. She felt better, the most rested she'd been since her arrival. She wondered if Thane had sent some of his healing power into her again, masking it with pleasuring her, healing her in stages. Maybe he'd not entered her because he knew she still needed to heal, that her trek with Deon had tired her more than she cared to admit.

She added another quality to the list that described Thane—not only was he strong and gentle, but he was shrewd.

Deon snorted once, scrubbed his face, then opened his dark eyes and focused them on her. "Hey."

"Hey yourself." A quick glance around the room told her they were alone, no servants in sight. Sunlight poured through high arched windows, bathing the room in liquid light.

"Thane's off doing king things," Deon said. "He told me to look after you."

"You can do that while snoring?"

Deon grinned. "I'm a man of many talents."

"You love him."

Deon's grin deserted him, his dark eyes quiet. "I never denied that. I thought it was obvious."

"I meant what I said in the caves—I have no intention of coming between you. I won't take him away from you."

He looked puzzled. "Take him away where?" His brow cleared and he bellowed a laugh that shook the bed. "Do you mean am I worried he'll *leave* me for you?" He rolled onto his back and laughed some more, until Lea flushed in confusion.

"I told you, we're sacred-bonded. If he bonds with you, I do too. We come as a set, love. All sacred-bonded men do."

Lea propped herself on her elbow. "Let me understand. Are all men sacred-bonded to each other? What about women?"

"Not every man is sacred-bonded to another man. Or a woman to a woman. But when they do sacred-bond, they're a pair forever. They can take other lovers, but they take lovers only together. It's simple."

"But doesn't the pair ever break up? For instance, if one falls in love with a third, but the other doesn't, and the new two want to be alone?"

He shook his head, blue beads clinking. "You still don't understand. We share a *sacred-bond*. We swear in front of priests and the world that we'll be loyal to each other until death. You don't enter a sacred-bond if you plan to ditch your partner as soon as you meet someone you want all to yourself. You agree to share everything—and I mean everything."

"Oh." She paused, trying to take it in. "What if you stop loving each other?"

"What kind of a hell-place do you come from? Is everyone like you beyond the Warding?"

"No." Lea sat up, wrapped her arms around her knees. "I'm just trying to understand. I've seen couples stay together for decades, but I've also seen them split up. We call it divorce."

Deon heaved a sigh, as though having to retain patience with a particularly dense child.

"Couples split up here too, but not ones who sacred-bond. You don't enter a sacred-bond unless you love the other person deeply and are willing to give him your life. You have to be a couple for at least seven years and prove your loyalty and your love in all kinds of ways. You don't do it unless you're damned sure."

So it was like a step beyond marriage—a deeper commitment for those who already believed their marriage sound. "And no sacred-bonded pair has ever broken up? *Ever?*"

"No!" He said it adamantly, his voice ringing to the ceiling. He put his hand over his face, shaking his head.

She gave him a quiet look. "I must sound arrogant and naïve to you. Go ahead, laugh at me."

Deon lowered his hand, his smile broad. "You are so damned cute. No wonder Thane likes you."

"It scares me how far from home I am," she said softly. "And really, it's not that far. A few light years is all I'd flown before the empire's finest blew me out of the sky."

Deon's smile vanished. "And I'd like to get my hands on whoever tried to hurt you."

"Would you?" She felt sudden mirth. "I'd love to see that."

The slender, over-teched, soft-skinned imperial officers who grew up on nutrition cubes and never had to do anything physical would fall over at the sight of Deon, a very physical male. He could crush them in his palm without breaking a sweat.

The problem was, the Four-One-Six Empire didn't need to fight with their hands. They had the best technology in the known galaxy and a planet like this was so much meat.

Whoever had shot her down had seen her not as a young woman in a scout ship desperately defending her home, but as a blip on a holo-screen, a colored dot. One techie had put out his pinkie and erased her.

And here she was. In bed with Deon, the most powerful male she'd ever met, except for Thane.

Deon sat up and threw back the covers. "Bath time." His eyes twinkled. "Join me?"

"If it's going to be anything like last night's bath, I might not have the strength."

He sprang out of bed, fresh and rested, his hard body a delight to watch. His cock was at half-mast, his hands on narrow hips, every muscle sculpted to male perfection. Even the fighting scars on his body only enhanced him, as did the lion tattoos that streamed down his arm and across his abdomen.

"I'll go easy on you. I'll soap you down, you soap me down—we'll see what happens."

Her heart beat faster. "What about Thane? Aren't you supposed to be at his side twenty-four/seven?"

Deon frowned as he tried to puzzle out her idiom. "I have to sleep sometimes. And bathe and eat. I have backup. Besides, Thane says you're more important and I believe him." He snatched the covers from her body, his grin returning. "Come on. Thane expects us for the midday meal and then you're getting your tattoos."

She gulped a little at the reminder. "I'll be right there."

Deon shrugged and headed for the bathroom, giving her a nice view of his firm ass as he went. The man was a walking sex god.

Lea got out of bed and stretched, unkinking muscles. She felt good, almost back to her normal strength. The mirror across the room showed her hair a complete blonde-and-brown mess and her face creased by the sheets. Terrific. No wonder Deon laughed at her.

She pulled on a silk robe that had been left for her by the bed and went to the dresser in search of a hairbrush.

A huge splash came from the bathroom. "Water's great. Come on in."

"Coming."

She saw a movement in the mirror and turned with a gasp, but it was only Emilie stepping out from behind a curtain. Had she been there the whole time? Maybe Deon's idea of a joke?

No, there was a door behind the curtain. The courtesan had just come in, smiling her charming smile. "I apologize for startling you," she said in a low voice.

"No problem. How was your daughter's birthday?"

Emilie's eyes warmed. "Quite lovely. She was enchanted by Lord Thane's gift."

"What was it? If you don't mind my asking."

Emilie brightened at her interest. "I don't mind at all. I'll show you." She reached into her robe, revealing her slender arms covered with the pretty tattoos. Lea stepped next to her, expecting pictures of some kind, but Emilie pulled out a small silk pillow, like a sachet.

"What's that?"

"A pretty thing my daughter gave me." She lifted it to Lea's nose and as Lea bent down, Emilie shoved the pillow into her face.

Lea caught an odor similar to that of an herb her own people used as an anesthetic. Black spots swam in front of her eyes and she held her breath and pushed Emilie away.

Emilie's pleasant smile vanished. She came at Lea again with the pillow, but Lea elbowed the other woman hard. Emilie gurgled and stumbled but was up before Lea could drag in a cleansing breath.

Courtesans must have fighting training, she thought as Emilie darted in, wiry and strong. *Or maybe gymnastics lessons.*

She tried to call for Deon, who was splashing noisily in the next room, but all that came from her was a croak.

Emilie was utterly silent. Lea swept her foot around and dragged Emilie's legs out from under her. Emilie's eyes blazed as she grabbed Lea, pulling her down with her.

Lea fought. The pillow skittered across the room. Lea scrambled out from under Emilie and shouted as loud as she could for Deon.

The big man moved fast, out of the water and through the door before the echoes of her cry died away. He plunged toward them, ready to defend her, not even sparing time for amazement.

Emilie wrapped her arms around Lea. She held a device Lea recognized, the transport button from her own ship. It only worked if the device inside her ship worked—the button homed her back to the device.

How does Emilie know about a transport button and how it works? was her thought as buzzing filled her ears.

She heard Deon's roar, which dissolved into the gentle tinkling of livestock bells, and she landed somewhere dark on a hard dirt floor.

Chapter Eight
Answers

℘

"What the hell happened?"

Thane tried to keep his voice steady as he faced a leather armor-clad Deon in the antechamber of the council room. A messenger had slipped in to whisper to Thane that Deon needed to speak to him most urgently.

Urgent meant something to do with either Lea or Felin. Thane had curtly told his councilors, who ranged in age from a young man of twenty to a woman of a venerable ninety-two, that he'd return and followed the messenger out.

Deon knew better than to announce dire news at the top of his lungs in the crowded council hall, hence the messenger. Deon's eyes betrayed his rage and worry as he related in a low voice that Lea and Emilie had disappeared.

Thane strode grimly from the antechamber down halls to a more private room, Deon moving swiftly and silently beside him.

"Disappeared how? How could they get past the twenty guards on every door? How did they get past *you?*"

No one got past Deon. The man could rise from a sound sleep and have his dagger to the throat of an intruder in the blink of an eye. Thane had not worried in the slightest leaving Lea in Deon's care.

"I mean she *disappeared*. She and Emilie. One second there, the next gone. They just—dissolved."

"Emilie was taken too?"

"Emilie took her. I think. Lea was fighting her and then *poof,* they were gone."

"How is that possible?" Thane demanded. "No magic can do that."

"How the hell should I know? I only know what I saw."

Thane threw off the ornate velvet cloak he'd donned for the council meeting, finding the folds suddenly stifling. "The palace is being searched?"

"Even as we speak. And the grounds and the streets beyond and the whole damn city. No one has reported anything positive and no one saw them."

"Gods damn Felin." His heart hammered fast and hard. "If he hurts her…"

"You're sure it was Felin?"

"Who else? And why was Emilie fighting her? How did Emilie get in to see her?"

"She's not barred from your chamber. The guard let her pass, like he always does. *I* would have let her pass."

"Where's Balin?" Thane asked sharply.

The fact that the courtesans could betray him twisted like a knife. They'd proved their loyalty again and again, but the penalty for betrayal of the king—of the clan—was death. *It comes to this – to save my kingdom, I have to kill my friends.*

"Balin I found. My guards say he was wandering the halls and they arrested him. He's in the library. I thought you'd like to talk to him before we haul him off."

Thane shot him a hard look, spun on his heel and left the room.

His heart pounded with fear and anger as he made for the library in the lower hall. His beautiful palace suddenly seemed menacing, all those rooms and corridors and arched galleries that could hide Lea from him. His enemies had skulked among them and abducted Lea the first chance they got.

Disappeared, dissolved. It made no sense. No magic could do that—but maybe technology could. He thought back to the strange devices he'd taken from Lea and her ship, none of

111

which he understood. Her weapon could slice a rock in two according to Deon. Had another weapon turned Lea, and Emilie, to dust?

No. Gods, no.

He needed Lea, and not just because she might be his salvation. He needed her, with those beautiful jade-green eyes, her multi-hued hair, her lopsided smile, her hardheaded practicality warring with her amazement at the ordinary things of Pamaar.

A woman who'd fallen from the sky in a strange device and survived, whose home was now unreachable, who spoke with common sense and healthy skepticism, who was afraid of drakes and astonished that both he and Deon wanted her.

His anger had reached a boiling point by the time he slammed into the library.

The peace of the place, the calm of rows of books reaching to the ceiling, was tainted by the presence of the guards in leather, men whose violence boiled just below the surface. They encircled Balin, who stood white-faced with fear.

The line of guards broke as Thane strode into the room, followed by Deon. Deon unsheathed his knife, stepped to Balin and pressed the blade to Balin's throat.

"Where is Emilie and where is Lea?" he asked.

Balin went whiter still. "I have no idea. Lea is missing? And Emilie? No one will explain what has happened."

He swallowed as Deon pressed the knife a little tighter to his skin. "Tell me about Emilie."

"What do you mean? Tell you what?"

Thane could see the fear in Balin's aura as black threads around his body. As a healer, Thane's instinct was to soothe him, but if Balin had betrayed them...

Balin's position was one of the most trusted in the kingdom, the one man who could get closer to the king than even the man with whom he'd sacred-bonded.

Whoever had made the law had been shortsighted. The law said Thane couldn't be with the man he loved in the way he wanted, but allowed him to have a substitute—a substitute Thane wouldn't become emotionally attached to and who could be disposed of if things went wrong.

Laws knew nothing about love, nothing about friendship or trust. Laws kept Thane from the man who would die for him and put him in the hands of ones who would sell him out.

"Back off a little, Deon," Thane said in a quiet voice. "Let me talk to him."

If anything, Balin looked more fearful. Deon glanced at Thane, then made a show of shrugging and moving away, as if to say to Balin *You think I'm scary...*

Thane gestured for Balin to sit. The courtesan took a chair at the table, the guards still flanking him. Balin was dressed as he had been the night before, in a sleeveless silk tunic that hugged his body and showed off his hard biceps and interlaced tattoos.

Thane stood over him, keeping his pose unthreatening but stern. "Tell me Emilie's plans."

Balin's eyes were wide. "I don't know her plans. She's been worried and tired lately, but she hasn't said anything to me. Her daughter is ill."

"I know." Thane felt grim. Emilie's daughter had the same kind of sickness that had killed Cerena. Emilie had brought the little girl to Thane for curing and Thane hadn't been able to help much.

"I swear to you, I know nothing about Lea," Balin said. "Emilie hasn't talked to me—I never see her outside the palace. I go home to my partner and wife and children when you don't need me. I swear this."

"We can verify that, you know," Deon rumbled. "Anyone who touches Thane is watched *twenty-four/seven,* as Lea says."

Thane held up his hand. "Wait. I think he's telling the truth."

Balin looked hopeful. Thane's healing sense could see past the black threads of fear to the white and golden threads of the man's heart, which were untainted by guilt.

"Tell me everything you know about Emilie," he said.

"I know very little about her. We work together, but as I said, I never see her when we leave. We go our separate ways. She goes home to her daughter—at least I assume she does."

"And you've never seen her with someone from the falcon-sword clan?"

"No, never. She's loyal to you. She must be. She's lion-star."

"But the lion-star king weakens," Thane said, his tone ironic. "Hadn't you heard?"

A few guards shifted uncomfortably and earned a quelling glare from Deon.

Balin shook his head. "That doesn't matter to me, my lord. I'm lion-star. I will fight beside you until the end."

Deon still wasn't satisfied. "Then what were you doing skulking around the halls?"

Balin looked startled. "Skulking? I was waiting to see if you'd send for me again. I hadn't been dismissed."

"That's true," Thane said. "I never sent him home."

Deon threw him a look. "You believe him?"

"One thing you learn when you are king is when to believe someone and when to doubt." He laid his hand on Balin's shoulder. "He is telling the truth."

Deon still scowled, but he wouldn't question Thane's judgment in front of the guards.

"Then that means he doesn't know what happened to Lea," Deon pointed out.

"No, but I can guess." Thane straightened up. "If she's alive, Felin has her—and I am going to get her back."

* * * * *

Lea lay facedown on hard-packed earth, her arms pinned behind her and tied. They'd gagged her as well but hadn't blindfolded her, not seeming to mind if she looked around.

She was in a large tent made of sturdy canvas held up by finely carved wooden poles. Her heart skipped a beat as she recognized the carvings, the same as on the stick one of Felin's men had poked her with after her crash landing.

The falcon symbols stood out, the fierce bird with its severe beak, beautiful in its wildness. The artistry was amazing, every feather carved to perfection, and it was only a tent pole.

The canvas flaps parted and the falcon-sword clan leader, Felin, entered. He looked the same as when he'd pried her from her ship—studded leather vest that bared his chest, falcon tattoos on his cheeks, his arms covered with sword tattoos. Dark eyes, brown hair, silver earring and her own bloodstone, her good-luck charm, hanging around his neck.

She scowled at him and started swearing through the cloth in her mouth.

Two guards entered behind him and flanked Lea. Emilie emerged last, looking both sad and ashamed.

"Sorry, I can't summon any sympathy for you," Lea growled at Emilie through the gag.

Felin dropped to one knee and slid the cloth from her mouth. "Do you understand me?"

"You are a dung-faced, pox-rotted, mother-loving, scrag-breathed—"

"I will take that to mean *yes*."

"You took my transport button, you bastard."

"An interesting device," Felin said. "We studied and tested the things we took from your ship, and found this little button most useful."

"Only until the power runs out. And anyway, I thought technology was illegal on this rock. *Verboten.*"

"Using the device was necessary—Thane has you too well-guarded. Even when you flew out with Deon and let him screw you in the Warding caves, we couldn't get near you."

Lea masked her surprise. She hadn't seen Deon's guards any more than she'd seen Felin's falcon-sword warriors, but she should have guessed that Deon wouldn't leave the city without serious backup.

"So what is your dastardly plan?" Lea asked. "You're supposed to rub your hands and say *I have you now, my pretty.*"

He cocked his brow. "Am I? In truth, I had no plan. I only wished to get you away from Thane and determine why you are here and what you mean for Pamaar."

"Why are any of us here?" Lea countered. "It's life. Stuff happens Not always for a purpose."

"You don't think so? The king's power fails and suddenly a fireball drops from the sky containing a young woman with devices we've never seen before. A coincidence?"

"Yes." Lea rolled herself to a sitting position, every limb aching. "The Warding is some kind of shield, isn't it, keeping people off this planet and hiding it from all readouts? It's the best baffler shield I've ever seen and I have no idea how it works—but hey, it works."

Felin shook his head. "It is not what you call *technology.*"

"No technology I've ever seen, I agree. It's either highly advanced or something natural, part of the planet. Anyway, the shield is starting to fail for some reason and I fell through a chink in it. People pass this planet by all the time—I just happened to get shot to hell above it. Coincidence."

"And you just happened to find the chink. Most would interpret that as a gift from the gods. Or a sacred quest led by your bloodstone." He touched the pendant around his neck, unapologetic for stealing it.

"I'm the least of your worries," Lea said. "If that shield goes down, you're all sitting ducks, no matter what clan you belong to. The empire will find Pamaar in two seconds flat."

"The evil darkness from beyond the Warding?" Felin's lips quirked.

"You call it evil darkness, I call it the Four-One-Six Quad Empire—same thing. It's trying to harvest my planet and if it finds yours, you're all toast."

Felin watched her narrowly. "That is why the king must die. He fails, and the Warding fails. They are linked. He will bring chaos upon us."

"Maybe it's the other way around. He's failing because the Warding is. Have you ever thought it might not be his fault?"

Felin smiled slightly, then he reached down and brushed a finger across her cheek. "He has thoroughly charmed you, hasn't he? Thane can be quite charming, Emilie tells me."

Lea spared a glance for Emilie, who flushed. "So you're ready to chuck Thane aside? Why not help him repair the Warding instead?"

"The Warding will be repaired when I am king," Felin said in a hard voice. "I will bind with it and my strength will restore it."

"You're optimistic. Not to mention egotistical."

"My people are dying. Thane can do nothing. There is no other choice."

His eyes glittered with anger and his hands clenched. He was a man frustrated, wanting to act.

Lea could almost feel sympathy—except that he'd kidnapped her and tied her up and was determined to kill Thane.

"What I think is that the rules have changed," she said. "You have so many rules, which you usually follow without question." She thought of Deon's surprise when he explained that no one would dream of going to the forbidden Warding caves, even though they were left unguarded. "And now there are questions."

Felin's frown told her she'd hit a mark. "And you are the biggest question. What are you?"

She shrugged. "I'm just a scout from the Rock."

"Now you will be Lea of the Falcon-Sword Clan."

"I don't think so..."

Felin turned away and snapped his fingers. The tent flaps parted again and a young man entered carrying a wooden box and a roll of cloth. He knelt beside Felin and spread out the scarlet cloth, then opened the box. Inside lay a neat row of needles of different sizes and pots of many and varied colors of ink.

"No. Oh no, no, no."

Lea tried to scramble away, but a guard stopped her with his boot. Felin's smile returned. He crouched next to her and yanked open her robe, clinically looking over every inch of her bare flesh while she lay bound and immobile.

He touched the curve of her hip. "The first one here. A falcon. And then a sword all the way down her neck." He traced from her chin to the hollow of her throat and Lea squirmed in earnest.

The tattoo artist noted her fear in surprise. "I will not hurt you, my lady."

"That's not the point."

"Put her to sleep," Felin snapped. "You'll never be able to work with her moving around so much."

The tattoo artist looked startled again but reached for one of the larger needles. He dipped it into a ceramic vial and Lea kicked out, her scout's training letting her land a blow on the tattoo artist's arm.

Felin snatched the needle as it fell out of the man's hand and quickly and precisely plunged it into Lea's side. She drew two breaths, stared accusingly at Emilie, who had watched the entire process in anguish, then succumbed to darkness.

* * * * *

Lea struggled again to wakefulness to find herself on a camp bed filled with soft cushions and pillows. She still wore her robe, but her bonds had been removed. She lay still for a moment, thoughts fuzzy and uncertain, then she gasped and sat up, head spinning.

Someone stirred in the shadows on the other side of the tent. Lea recognized Emilie as she rose sinuously from a couch and moved to Lea.

Lea braced herself to fight, but her limbs were saggy and weak, probably from whatever drug had knocked her out. No wonder they hadn't bothered to keep her tied.

Emilie sat down at the edge of the bed and reached for Lea as though she would hug her.

"Don't even touch me," Lea said sternly.

Emilie let her arms fall, her expression sad. "I am sorry. It was the only way."

She did look sorry. Grief-stricken, even.

"So now I'm branded as a falcon-sword," Lea growled. "I thought the choice was mine. So much for the rules." She touched her throat, trying to feel the tattoo.

Emilie shook her head. "They only did one, on your hip. The falcon."

Lea shoved back covers to see her hip covered with an intricately feathered bird, a falcon with wings outstretched. One wing came forward over her hipbone, the other fanned out to her buttock. Any other time, she might think it pretty and marvel at the workmanship.

"Damn him."

Emilie reached for Lea again, this time stopping when she lightly brushed Lea's hand. "I'm sorry. I wanted things to be different."

Lea realized that the other woman gazed at Lea's body in sad longing and Lea sighed and dragged her robe closed. "Things couldn't have been different. I prefer men."

Emilie's touch turned caressing. "I could show you."

"Not after you tried to drug me and then brought me here by force. I thought all lion-stars were fanatically loyal to their clan. To Thane."

Tears beaded on Emilie's dark lashes. "It was the only way. If Felin has you and you are falcon-sword, he can more quickly persuade others to let him take over as king. He promised me that Lord Thane does not have to die, but can live in exile—as long as he is able."

"And you believed him?"'

"He promised me. He gave me his word, sworn on a bloodstone."

"*My* bloodstone. He stole it when he found me."

"The fact that you wore it means you were on a sacred quest," Emilie said. "Everyone will believe your sacred quest is to restore Pamaar and give the people their rightful king."

"Yes. *Thane.* Anyway, can you see Deon and Thane bowing their heads and saying, *You're right, Felin, here's the kingdom, we're leaving?*"

She shook her head. "No."

"What are you getting out of all this? Money?"

Emilie stood up, indignant. "No. I would never betray my clan for payment."

"What then?"

Emilie deflated. She was an attractive woman, but not overwhelmingly beautiful. It was her smiles and her warmth that made her seem beautiful, a woman every man's gaze would follow. "It would be simpler if I showed you."

She glided away and out of the tent before Lea could say anything more. Lea's limp muscles wouldn't let her move and she lay unhappily until Emilie returned.

Emilie led a child by the hand, a girl of about seven or eight years. The girl was muffled in a cloak although the weather was warm.

"Reana," Emilie said softly. "This is Lea, the lady who fell to Pamaar like a star."

Reana's eyes were huge in her small face. She looked up at Lea in wonder, showing tiny lion tattoos on her cheekbones. She was adorable.

"Hello, Reana," Lea said. "Would you like to sit with me?"

Reana nodded without speaking and scrambled into Lea's lap. Lea closed her arms around the girl, who smelled like soap, as though she'd just bathed. She was very trusting, which told Lea that Reana had no idea what intrigue Emilie had dragged her into.

Giving Lea a sad look, Emilie gently brushed back Reana's cloak.

Lea gasped. The little girl's skin was mottled as though it had been burned and was an unhealthy grayish pink. Her nails were brittle and some gone, her hair crackling and dry. Most of all, Lea read misery in the girl's eyes, a wilting of her zest for life, a child sensing she was dying.

Lea looked up at Emilie in shock and sympathy. "How did this happen?"

Emilie shook her head as she arranged the folds of Reana's silk cloak to cover her head and face. "I don't know. She began taking ill months and months ago. Lord Thane could not cure her and she has grown steadily worse."

"He *can't* cure her," Lea said. "Not of this."

She set Reana on the bed and got to her feet. Her legs wobbled uncontrollably and she had to grab Emilie for support. "Damn, what was in that Mickey?"

"Mickey?" Emilie asked, startled.

"Never mind. Emilie, Thane might not be able to cure your daughter, but I can. But I have to get back to Thane's palace to do it."

Emilie's eyes narrowed in suspicion. "How can you? You have no healing power, no affinity with the Warding."

"No, but I have a few tricks of my own. I can't really explain, but I swear to you, if you get me out of here and back to the palace, I'll help Reana." She drew a long breath, pieces of the puzzle falling into place. Now to see if she could get out of here safely and find out if she was right before it was too late.

Chapter Nine
Challenge

છ

Thane led the phalanx, even though he could feel Deon glowering from where he rode behind Thane in the saddle. But Thane couldn't sit in the palace twiddling his thumbs while Deon and his men rushed to Lea's rescue.

Felin would not kill him outright while the laws were still in place, nor would any of his men. Thane would have to be formally Challenged and the time and place set for the combat, or the Pamaarans would tear Felin apart. Even Felin's own clan wouldn't be able to help him if he violated the most sacred of laws.

It had taken five hours to fly from the city to the valley where Felin waited. Felin had taken to camping on the very edge of Thane's territory, ready to march to the city at a moment's notice.

A circle of tents came into view, colorful canvases and banners flapping in the wind, the falcon symbol prominent. Deon gave a signal and the contingent of drakes dove in formation to land just inside lion-star territory.

Felin was there to meet them, of course. He carried a flag with a gold cross on a red background, the flag of truce.

"Truce," Deon growled in Thane's ear. "Because he knows I'll tear his head off if I get near him."

Thane was ready to do some head tearing as well. He leapt from his drake and strode to meet Felin.

Guards from both clans encircled the two of them, glaring suspiciously at one another. Falcon-sword banners snapped in the wind, as did the lion-star's behind Thane.

"Thane of Lion-Star," Felin began in a clipped voice. "I Challenge you to defend the throne of Pamaar, by—"

"The hell you do," Deon broke in. "You abducted a woman under Thane's protection and broke the law."

Felin turned a hard gaze on Deon. "I'm not talking to you, guard dog. And Thane is the one who's broken the law. The woman was mine, under *my* protection, until you stole her from me."

"She seems happy with us. Funny, she never tried to run back to you—you had to steal her. She's lion-star now."

Felin raised one brow. "The only tattoo I saw on Lea is that of a falcon."

Deon clenched his fists. "It's a crime against all Pamaar to force someone into a clan."

Felin smiled. "She didn't resist."

Deon started forward. Thane put one hand on his chest to hold him back. Deon fumed but remained in place.

"I accept your Challenge," Thane said to Felin. "On the condition that you return Lea to me."

Felin's smile widened. "What if she doesn't want to go?"

"She can make the choice. But only after I have seen that she is not hurt and that she is truly allowed to make her own decision."

"You'd let her go?" Felin gave him an incredulous look.

"If she wished." Thane's heart burned, but he'd never had any intention of keeping her with him against her will. "Bring her to me and we'll discuss the Challenge."

Felin's eyes shone in triumph. He snapped his fingers and gave an order to a man with swirled blue tattoos on his face. The man nodded and trotted away through the falcon-sword ranks.

Thane wondered if Felin would truly let Lea go, or what scheme the man had in mind. The Challenge was sacred and once Felin offered it, he could not be harmed, but Thane had no qualms against snatching Lea back from him if necessary.

"You choose the time and place," Felin was saying to Thane. "Since you are the Challenged. Within two seven-nights, of course."

"I will debate with my council about the most auspicious time. And I choose the plain before the Warding caves. That way whoever emerges as king will not have far to travel for the binding."

"Done."

Blue-tattoo man came running back. "Sir," he said breathlessly, his eyes round in distress. "She's gone."

Felin gave him an impatient look. "What?"

"The woman, sir. She's gone. She's escaped, and so has the courtesan and her child."

* * * * *

Lea's stomach rolled as the drake plummeted again, his erratic flying making her nauseous. But they had to stay behind the line of hills and within the treetops to avoid detection, which meant some tricky flying.

Emilie rode the drake competently. The slender courtesan had been the one to harness and saddle the drake under cover of darkness and then to help Lea and Reana mount.

Lea still felt weak and ineffectual, whatever drug Felin had plunged into her still in her system. She wore a short cloak Emilie had found for her over the silk robe she'd shrugged on in Thane's bedroom, but it was a little protection against the night wind.

Reana rode in front of Lea, confidently snuggling into her. Lea had to trust that Emilie would take them back to Thane's palace. She had a good sense of direction, but without charts and with little light, she had no idea where they were and her lingering grogginess didn't help.

Lea had wanted Emilie to fetch the transport button plus the main device that had been torn out of her ship, but Emilie had negated that plan.

"Felin has everything he stole from you in his tent, which is well-guarded." She'd looked doubtful. "If I could get it, would it help us? Would it take us to Thane's palace?"

Lea shook her head with regret. "The button only takes you to where the device is. It's not a two-way transport. It was for emergencies—in case I got lost or captured while out of my ship, I could transport back to it and get my butt out of there."

Emilie's look said she didn't really understand, but it didn't matter, because she had no way of getting past the guards and into Felin's tent. She explained that a courtesan had to wait to be summoned and if she simply showed up claiming to want to pleasure Felin, he was sure to be suspicious.

Reluctantly, Lea agreed to leave it behind. Emilie got them to the drake pens, then guided the drake tight and low behind the hills, out of sight of any search parties.

Or so Lea thought. As they flew over a ridge to see the nearing lights of the city, the air was suddenly full of drakes. They came from every which way, quickly surrounding Emilie's drake, screeching their triumph.

One beast dove for them like an arrow, wings folded, neck outstretched. Lea bit back a scream as Emilie's drake swerved sharply to avoid it. The other drake flew in a tight circle around them, driving them, but Lea couldn't see who was on its back through the flurry of wings and dust.

Emilie landed in a flat meadow just outside the city gates and they dismounted, drakes settling down around them. The drake that had chased them thumped to the ground and Lea recognized Cutie even before Deon slid off his back and stormed over.

Deon had his sword out, a gleaming length of bronze. Emilie paled and Reana whimpered and clung to her mother's robes.

Lea stepped between Emilie and Deon. "Wait. Just wait."

"Are you all right?" he demanded. "Get out of the way—I need to arrest her."

"Not yet. Can you wait a minute? Where's Thane?"

"Right here." Thane's strong hands spun her around and suddenly she found herself in his arms. He held her, tight, tight, then he cupped her face in his hands.

"I thought I'd lost you," he breathed, then said fiercely. "Did he hurt you? If he touched you, I'll tear him apart, to hell with the Challenge."

Challenge? What Challenge? Lea wanted to ask, but there were too many other things to take care of.

"Nothing that will scar me for life," she said quickly. *Well, except the tattoo.* "I need the things you took from me—my ration bars and ident card and everything. Please say you still have them."

Thane looked mystified. "As I told you, they are under guard."

"I need them." She locked her fingers around his arms. "Please."

He glanced at Emilie and the courtesan flinched and wouldn't meet his eyes.

"She did what she did for a good reason," Lea said. "Her daughter is sick."

Thane's mouth flattened. Deon looked ready to explode, his scowl dark.

"This is not the place to discuss it," Thane said.

"Fine." Lea gathered her robe tightly over her bare body. "Can we go inside and discuss it, then? *With* Emilie?"

Thane glanced from her to Deon to Emilie and back again, and finally gave a nod.

Deon seized Emilie by the shoulder. "You ride with me. We'll get someone to look after your daughter."

Reana made a noise of distress and clung to her mother. Lea went to her, touched her. "It's all right, sweetie. We're going to the palace and I'll be there." She straightened up and looked at Deon. "Reana can ride with Emilie, can't she, Deon?"

Deon's lip curled and she saw a gleam of exasperation in his eyes. "Yes, all *right*."

Thane held Lea in front of him on the drake, his arm around her protectively. The drake jerked into the air and within minutes settled down into the palace grounds.

Thane walked close to her as they made their way to his private quarters, his hand on her shoulder as though he didn't want to break contact with her. He took her to the opulent room in which Lea had first awakened, then beyond to a smaller study, where a guard stood next to a locked cabinet.

Deon made Emilie sit in the main room while he hovered nearby with his sword. Reana sat on her mother's lap, her face buried in Emilie's bosom. Thane closed the door on them and went to the cabinet.

He opened it with a key from around his neck. Lea's equipment lay on velvet-lined shelves as though they were museum pieces. When Lea reached for a slim cylindrical tube, Thane stopped her with his hand on her wrist.

"Why do you want it?"

"I can help Reana with this," Lea said, lifting the tube from the velvet. She touched the base and looked at the readout—still a full dose.

"I can *help* Reana too." Thane's eyes flickered with anguish and bitterness. "I can relieve some of the pain, but I can't cure her. I've tried. Broken bones and hurts like you had, yes, but not the kind of sickness Reana has."

"But I can cure her," Lea said.

"How? You are not a healer. I've seen your aura—you have none of the powers of the Warding."

"I know that. I also know what's wrong with her." She held up her hands as he started to speak again. "I'll explain everything later. But I know what's wrong with you, why you can't cure this disease, why the Warding let me through and why your wife died and you couldn't help her."

* * * * *

Thane tried to keep his emotions in check as he and Lea returned to the receiving room where Emilie and Reana and Deon waited.

So much tumbled in his brain—relief that Lea was safe, anger at Emilie, pity for her daughter, anger again at Felin for using Emilie, sadness that he'd have to punish her and impatient curiosity at Lea's claims. How could she cure the incurable and how could she understand what was wrong with the Warding when she was not even of Pamaar?

Lea had whispered that she thought the two of them should heal Reana together, Lea with her mysterious silver cylinder and Thane to soothe with his healing touch. He agreed it would be best for Reana, but Lea didn't understand when he tried to explain the implications to her.

If he and Lea healed Reana together—not that he believed they could—people would believe he'd given Lea some of his healing powers. Lea saw nothing wrong with this, but Thane would have as good as proclaimed her his queen. And with Felin having issued the Challenge, things could get sticky.

"I don't understand your politics," Lea had told him, her green eyes innocent and adamant. "But I understand a little girl is suffering—needlessly. Let me do this."

Her compassion flared warmth through his heart and he kissed her with feeling. "Reana won't have to pay for the stupidity of the rest of us," he whispered against her hair. "Don't worry."

"But you'll pay," Lea said.

"I am king." He kissed her again and sent her a smile. "It's what I do."

He took her hand and they walked into the outer room together.

Emilie's face was nearly gray as she watched Thane approach, fear and guilt stark in her eyes. She well knew the penalty for betraying her clan and the fact that she'd had to risk death to help her daughter nearly killed him.

Lea, on the other hand, flushed with excitement. She sat down on the sofa and patted her lap for Reana to come over.

Emilie released her daughter reluctantly, but Reana came to Lea with perfect trust. Thane had a sudden vision of Lea holding a child—*his* child but with Lea's green eyes. He wanted that with all the strength he possessed.

Lea pushed back Reana's cloak to bare one small arm. "This might sting a little."

"It won't." Thane sat on Reana's opposite side and took her other hand. "You'll feel nothing."

Reana believed him and readily stuck her arm out to Lea.

Lea touched the end of the gleaming cylinder to Reana's skin. Thane absorbed the brief pain as it entered her, a stinging flash as though he'd touched a thorn plant, then it was gone.

He kept his hand on Reana and soothed her, his healing sight observing the gray and black tangle of threads that was her strange disease, a tangle he'd never been able to unravel.

As he watched, a stream of light emanated from where Lea's cylinder had touched Reana. The light flowed to the threads and then suddenly began to surround and untangle them.

His healing sight let him see the threads solidify and become whole again, the sticky blackness changing to vibrant yellow and white. Health, not sickness. He lifted his gaze to Lea, who simply smiled at him.

Lea pulled the cylinder away. Reana studied her arm where the cylinder had touched it, but it had left no mark. But Thane saw that the lesions on her skin suddenly looked less raw.

Reana sat back as though nothing much had happened, a child expecting more excitement than she'd received. She looked over at her mother with clear brown eyes. "Mama, will you ask Lord Thane if I can go play with the drakes?"

Her voice was strong, the hoarse weakness she'd had for so long gone. Emilie burst into tears. Deon did not stop her as she hurried to the sofa and sank to her knees before it, gathering Reana in her arms. She continued to cry incoherently, burying her face in Reana's lap.

Reana looked down at her mother in surprise. "It's all right, Mama, I feel better today."

"What the hell did you do?" Deon demanded. The guards surrounding him looked just as stunned and impressed.

"The entire damage can't be reversed, of course," Lea said in a matter-of-fact voice. "She's been exposed for too long, but it can be stopped and much of it repaired. I'm sure if she has more healing sessions with Thane, she'll be fine."

The guards began to smile, star tattoos moving on their faces. They were too well-trained to speak, but Thane knew what they thought—*the king has regained his powers. Lion-stars are still on top.*

Only he hadn't. He stood up, took Lea by the arm and pushed her in front of him out of the room. He closed the door on Emilie's sobs and Deon's astonished expression and took Lea through the antechamber and to his private sleeping rooms.

The bath, which he'd ordered prepared for Lea on their arrival, steamed in readiness.

Thane released her and slung his cloak away. "Take off your clothes and get in."

131

Lea beamed a smile. "If this is your way of saying *thanks*, I like it." She started to remove the robe, then her smile vanished and she hesitated. "Um, maybe I should do this alone."

"Why?"

She sighed. "I guess you're going to find out sooner or later."

She laid the cylinder on a table, then turned her back to him and slid off the robe. Her body came into view a little at a time, slim shoulder blades, curve of back, tight backside...

With the wing of a falcon on it. She turned to the side to show him the bird drawn intricately across her hipbone, wings feathering to either side. His anger clenched him, hot and sparking.

"He told me," he said in a hard voice. "Did you choose?"

"No, he had the artist give me something to knock me out." She self-consciously touched her hip. "I feel violated. And confused."

Thane relaxed a fraction, but no more. "*Felin* has broken the laws, not you. Get into the bath."

Lea dropped the robe to the floor and slid into the water, not hiding her relief when the heat touched her. She looked over her shoulder at him in apprehension. "What are you going to do?" she asked.

"Wash you," he answered.

Chapter Ten
Offers

ℰↃ

He really meant it.

Thane, naked, splashed down beside her and scooped a handful of sweet-smelling soap from the jar on the edge of the bath. Then he proceeded to scrub her all over, first with a cloth, then a sponge, then his bare hands.

He washed her from neck to breasts, stomach, arms, hips, back and legs, rubbing vigorously as though trying to remove all traces of Felin's camp from her. He even rested her feet in his lap and scrubbed those thoroughly too.

"Thane," Lea said.

He didn't answer. He moved his hands to her hips, still scrubbing.

"Thane," Lea repeated. "It won't come off. It's a tattoo."

His dark glance flicked to her briefly. "I know."

"That's why I don't like tattoos. What if you hate it once you have it? Or worse, the man you're falling for hates it?"

The scrubbing slowed. "What man are you falling for?"

"I thought that was obvious. I don't expect anything in return, don't worry about that. When I told Deon I didn't mean to come between you two, he thought I was hysterically funny—as if I ever could. Second, I don't belong here. I'm a resourceful scout—I'll figure out a way to get rescued and make it back home."

Thane stilled. "You cannot leave."

"I'll be careful not to reveal this paradise when I do go. And you can trust me to keep my mouth shut—if I can even find the place again once you repair the Warding. I couldn't stand to see it destroyed."

"I mean you cannot leave because I want you to stay."

Lea stopped, her heart beating faster. "Why?" She laughed a little. "You can't mean you need more sex. You have Deon, not to mention courtesans at your beck and call. I've always been a plain vanilla girl—all this ménage and same-sex and playtime is new to me."

He moved beside her in a rush of water, cupping his hands around her face. "When I knew you were gone, that Felin had you, I would have killed anyone in my path to get to you."

"Really?" she asked, voice faint. "How he-man of you."

"I never understand what you say and I can never make you understand what I want."

Lea touched his face, liking the rough of his whiskers abrading her fingertips. He'd dropped everything to come to her rescue when he had far many more things to worry about than one lost woman.

"Maybe we should stop using words then," she whispered. "Except for me to say thank you for coming after me."

He answered with a kiss that melted her. She felt as though her body dissolved into the hot water, sliding and happy to drown. His mouth possessed her, brutal and taking, bruising her.

He slid his hand between her legs, his large palm lifting her and cradling her against him. She felt his strong grip on her wrist, guiding her to the hardness that jutted out to her.

"Take me," he whispered. "Stroke me."

Lea needed no persuasion. She ran her fingers along his shaft, finding the silken smooth tip, circling her fingertips around his flange. He made a noise in his throat and pulled her closer. "Faster," he urged.

She understood what he wanted. Plain vanilla or not, she knew what to do.

He leaned his head back against the lip of the tub, his blond hair dark with water, the dust washed clean from him. She kissed him as she worked him, their tongues tangling in rough strokes.

This amazing man was teaching her so much, not just what was possible in bed but what was possible in a relationship. At one time she'd thought that men who loved other men were bizarre, but what he and Deon shared went deeper than what she'd seen in many man-woman couples.

And his caring went further than his personal sex life. Thane lived close to the bone, understanding the pulse of his people, willing to sacrifice everything to save them. She understood why Deon loved him.

"Make love to me," she whispered. "Please."

"Not yet."

He was maddening. She was going to scream with need and he wasn't even touching her.

Thane stood up, water trickling from his wet skin. Lea lost her hold on his cock, but it didn't matter because he moved the beautiful thing to hang right in front of her face.

"Take me in your mouth," he said.

She'd wanted to do that the first time she saw him naked. She licked his navel to tease him, tasting the saltiness of him plus the tinny flavor of the bathwater.

His cock was large, skin stretched tight over his dark length. She saw, up close, what she'd not seen before—a tiny tattoo of a lion right across his tip.

"Didn't that hurt?" she gasped.

"Not a bit.

"That's right—you give the artists the ability to ink you pain-free."

"Do you like it?" His voice softened. "It would be worth the pain then."

Lea traced the delicate outline of the crouching lion. "I do like it."

She rubbed her tongue over the lion, then opened her lips and took him inside. She could make this lion feel good with her lips and her tongue, making him dance for Thane.

His hands found her hair, shaking from holding himself back. He parted his feet to let her explore all of him—his tight balls lifting under her palm, his wiry hair, the warmth of him. He tasted good and as she suckled him, he rocked his hips a little to enter her mouth.

She looked forward to tasting his seed, but just as she felt him building to bursting point, he moved quickly away and lifted her out of the tub.

Before she could express disappointment, he laid her on the pile of towels waiting at the side of the bath and stretched out on top of her, his dark eyes filled with hunger and need.

"I'll go slow," he promised.

"Slow is good. So is fast."

"I'm large and you are tight. Deon told me how tight you were."

She gave a little laugh. "Does he always kiss and tell?"

Thane's brows drew together. "He tells *me*. We share every detail of the woman we love—"

She held up her hand. "I was joking. Don't say *love*, it scares me."

"Why?" His voice was low, even fierce. "I want to love you, to give you everything you desire."

"Even if I desire the impossible?"

"Even then."

She lightly touched his face. "It's killing me not to have you inside me."

His tip nudged her opening, a blunt hardness that made her ache. "Are you certain you're ready for me?"

"I'll risk it."

"In that case..."

He smiled, his eyes warming, as he slid all the way inside.

* * * * *

Love. Beautiful. Mine.

Thane's thoughts dissolved as the beauty of her flowed around him. Deon hadn't been exaggerating when he'd said she was tight.

Tight, oh gods, I thought she'd squeeze me in half, Deon had said last night when they'd held each other next to the sleeping Lea. *She had me coming like I hadn't had it in years.*

Deon had squeezed Thane's bare cock in demonstration, but it was nothing to what Thane felt inside this woman.

She lifted her hips to take all of him, her face softening into pleasure and desire. Her beautiful green eyes regarded him with such warmth he wanted to melt. But not yet. First he wanted to remain hard and enjoy every inch of her.

He'd promised slow, but feeling her, seeing her face, surrounding himself with her scent, he couldn't help but push faster. His thoughts became incoherent—there was no thought, just the raw joy of joining with her.

He felt much the same way inside Deon, feeling the one he loved hard around him. Lea was different of course, all soft femaleness while Deon was brutal muscle.

He dimly sensed Deon enter the room as he moved his hips. Lea arched to him, fingers closing on his tight arms, sensing nothing but their lovemaking.

Deon was still dust-coated from their long ride to and from Felin's territory, the odor of sweat and leather clinging to him. Lea was clean and warm from the bath, her skin scented with delicate soaps.

He wanted both of them. He wanted both of them *now*.

Deon, still dressed, knelt next to them. "Hey, beautiful." He gently stroked Lea's hair. "You look like you're having fun."

She turned her head into his touch, kissing his hand, at the same time lifting her hips to meet Thane's thrusts, her face twisted with need. Her pussy pulsed around him and Deon stroked her hair again, his gaze intent on her.

"She's going to come," Deon said. "That's how she did it when I fucked her."

"Goddess," she moaned. Her nipples pinched into tight buds that scraped Thane's hand. The soft sounds she made drove him crazy, her body reaching for his and dragging him into her.

She locked her legs around his, her soles warm on his bare legs. Her incredible pussy kept on throbbing in short little bursts, tight, tighter, tighter.

"Is she squeezing you?" Deon said hoarsely. "Doesn't it feel fucking good?"

Thane was on top of her fully, his tongue in her mouth, their skin sliding against each other's with bathwater and sweat. Her come smelled so good, the golden threads of her aura bright with it.

She locked her arms around his neck and began sucking his tongue, her hips pounding against his, her sheath still strangling his cock.

He felt his coming a long way off, but he couldn't stop it. Deon stroked his back to his ass and whispered, "Yes."

Thane's seed shot out of him in a bright burst and he roared with it. She squealed beneath him, her body pressed so hard against his that their auras tangled.

Gods, yes, she's mine, mine, mine. Felin will die for touching her. I'll take his fucking Challenge and split him in half for taking her away from me.

He was shouting it, but the words were incoherent. He felt Deon behind him, the big man's leather-rough hands on his bare back, but Deon's touch was soothing, quieting. Beneath him, Lea looked at him with tired green eyes, her fingertips feather-light on his face.

The world started spinning more slowly, his heartbeat winding down, the threads of their auras untangling and withdrawing. Thane kissed her, his frenzy gentling, and she smiled sleepily at him.

"Thank you," she murmured. "That was terrific."

"Hell, yes."

Deon got to his feet beside them again and Thane looked up at him. "Don't go away."

"I'm not going anywhere."

Thane's cock was completely spent by now, but he felt himself harden again as Deon began unlacing his leather tunic. They'd known each other for so long that each knew exactly what the other wanted without words. So many years, but it never grew stale. With Deon, it was always new.

Lea pushed her hair from her eyes with a languid hand. "What happened to Emilie?"

"I arrested her," Deon said. He pulled the tunic off over his head, baring his hard chest dusted with wiry black hair.

"But—" Lea began.

"Before you start screeching at me, she's in a nice chamber with her daughter with servants to bring them whatever they need. If we didn't arrest her, Thane would look like he condoned clan betrayal. He can't afford to do that."

Thane gave her a reassuring kiss. "She'll have a trial." His voice rasped, his throat raw. "And I will make sure everyone knows she risked my wrath and clan law trying to save her daughter. She can't go unpunished, but she might escape the harshest penalties."

"I still want to know how you did that," Deon said to Lea. He stood and stripped off his leggings then watched them with hands on hips, his cock dark and thick. "Cured Reana, I mean."

"With technology," Thane told him.

"Oh. Not good."

Lea tried to frown, though her gaze was riveted to Deon's body. "It was an anti-radiation dose, meant to combat exposure to the worst radiation out there. It's done. I can't take it back."

"I don't want you to." Thane kissed her again, her lips warm and swollen. "What you did took courage."

"And balls," Deon agreed. "Except you obviously don't have any. I like what you do have though."

"You have the worst pickup lines, Deon," Lea told him.

Deon gave her a dark smile. "I don't know what *pickup lines* are, but I'm glad I can make you laugh." He shot Thane a look. "Think she's ready for both of us?"

"Not yet," Thane answered. Regretfully, but he didn't want her to be hurt.

Lea's eyes widened. "You mean at the same time? I'm still blown away by you two just being in the same room with me."

"She likes us," Deon said.

"I hope so," Thane answered.

Lea smiled up at Thane. "I do. I like you a lot."

Her smile made his in-no-way-sated cock hard as granite. He moved into her again, closing his eyes at the fine sensation.

"Hey," Deon growled. "What about me?"

"Come down here," Thane said.

Lea's eyes widened then grew interested as Deon knelt beside them on the towels, his long cock in delectable reach. The same unyielding rules that kept Thane from enjoying

Deon inside him prevented him from taking Deon in his mouth, but Lea could have him.

As Thane slid himself farther into her, he had the satisfaction of watching her lips close around his best friend's cock.

* * * * *

Thane stretched her incredibly, and even more incredible was Deon's huge cock nudging inside her mouth. He tasted dark and hot, and the bead of moisture on his tip made her thirst for more.

Thane rode her more slowly this time, but that just let her feel every inch of him. She tried to feel every inch of Deon with her tongue, but he was so damn big. She wished she could have them stand face to face and touch their cocks together while she measured them from balls to balls. Wouldn't she have fun with that?

The fantasy triggered her orgasm. A jolt of pleasure washed over her, but did Thane stop?

He raised her leg and pushed her bent knee to her chest, sliding in even deeper. Deon laughed and made his cock dance over her lips, teasing her to catch it.

She did catch it, sucking hard until his eyes widened and ropes of thick come flowed into her mouth, more than she could manage. It didn't matter, because Thane kissed her like a thirsty man, tasting his lover on her tongue.

Lea sensed a change in them both, excitement mounting to raw levels. She shivered in sudden cold when Thane left her exposed, but he gently pulled a towel over her body, then turned to Deon.

His lovemaking with Deon wasn't tender—it was rough and wild and neither bothered to be quiet about it. Deon laughed and screamed and talked so dirty that Lea, even used to living with soldiers, popped open her eyes to stare at him.

Thane rode him, his ass bunching and releasing as his penis disappeared into Deon's anus. Lea's pussy overflowed at the sight of Deon's cheeks wrapped around the base of Thane's cock, evidence of Thane deep inside him.

The twist of Thane's face and Deon's flow of words was more evidence. Lea put her hand to her quim, cupping it hard as Deon came and then Thane did too. Thane leaned down and licked the lion tattoo across Deon's back.

Both men thumped to the floor, panting hard, and Deon laughed, voice raw. "I think we shocked her."

"No," Thane said, smiling his beautiful smile at Lea. "I think she liked it."

I'm going to die right now, she thought. *I've had sex with both of them and watched them fuck each other and loved every minute of it.*

Thane spooned up beside her and kissed her forehead. "Sleep, Lea. You need it."

As he'd done before, Thane touched his fingers to her face and healing sleepiness crept over her limbs.

"Not fair," she mumbled and she heard Deon laugh before she fell into deep sleep.

She woke alone in a bed, finding a silk dressing gown laid out for her. She put it on quickly and rose, not liking the way her legs shook. All that sex on top of a journey on one of those drakes plus the drug Felin had given her wasn't doing her any favors.

But she could feel her bones whole and strong, the skin around the tattoo healed, her muscles relaxed. Thane was better than any sleeping dose ever invented.

She emerged from the bedroom and found herself in Thane's private sitting room. He sat at a table, her basic survival kit arrayed before him, his hands resting flat on the table as he looked at it.

He'd dressed in a sleeveless tunic and leggings, the silk outlining his hard muscles. Her heart gave a painful beat.

Thane glanced up as she entered, his look pensive. He took such intense joy in lovemaking, but it couldn't distract him very long from the problems at hand.

"I can't stop thinking about Reana," he said as she slid into a chair next to his. "I could never reach or change the disease, no matter how hard I tried." He lifted the stylus-thin metal cylinder. "Yet you cured her within seconds with your technology."

"Not seconds," Lea corrected him. "I stopped the poison from breaking down her system. It will take a while for her to heal completely, but she'll feel better right away."

He rolled the cylinder between his fingers. "Will this cure everyone with the disease? If so, I should use it."

"I thought technology was forbidden."

His gaze was remote. "Those laws are ancient, from before the time of the Warding, when such objects nearly wiped out our people, or so the legends go. But how can I deny healing to my people? Tell them *yes, there is a cure, but you can't have it because of something our ancestors decided?* What kind of a king would that make me?"

The anguish in his eyes pulled at Lea's heart. "It doesn't matter, anyway. There was only one full dose in the cylinder, enough for me alone—the idea is that you dose yourself then take your butt home and to the medics. I gave half to Reana because she's so small. This could cure another small child, but no more."

The cylinder made a soft *click* as Thane set it on the table. "Then it is no solution."

"No, but it's part of the solution." She wrapped her hands around his and rested them against her chest. "I wouldn't have known it would cure Reana if I didn't know what's wrong with her. It's radiation poisoning."

She said the words in triumph, but they obviously meant nothing to Thane.

"I can heal poisons," he said. "But I have never seen this."

"Of course you haven't, because you have your big technology ban. But *something* is out there in Pamaar creating a radiation cloud." She gestured at the window, as though it would reveal the problem. "You can't see it or hear it or smell it or feel it, but that doesn't mean it isn't deadly. We just have to pinpoint its source and get rid of it."

"Is that all?" Thane asked, his smile faint.

"Since Felin's people are most affected, I would guess the whatever-it-is is in his territory. Didn't your wife Cerena go to the falcon-sword clan to try to heal them? Find out exactly where she went—I'm betting she got massive dose if she got sick so fast."

"You are telling me that this *technology* is killing my people?"

"It might be natural—a radioactive metal suddenly being exposed or something. Your powers have weakened and I saw parts of the Warding black and dead. The Warding looks like a natural occurrence, something unique to Pamaar. When the radiation started interfering with it, your powers weakened." She thought a moment. "What *is* the Warding, exactly? I tried to look it up, but your library didn't have anything useful."

Thane shrugged. "It is—the Warding. When a clan leader becomes king, he goes to the Warding caves alone and the Warding binds with him and becomes one with him."

"And then when he comes out, he can heal everyone?"

"Yes. It happens sometimes that the binding is weak and the king dies quickly, but usually they live to a ripe old age and die surrounded by their grandchildren. But when the binding is weak, the leader of the upcoming clan can Challenge and try the binding himself. In this case, the falcon-sword clan is next in the ruling cycle and Felin has issued the Challenge."

"You have to let him kill you?"

"Not necessarily. If I prove to be the stronger physically, I can go to the caves and try the binding again. But if Felin wins, then he goes to the caves and becomes king."

Lea made a noise of exasperation. "It won't matter who wins if it's the Warding that's weak. Felin won't be able to bind either. It's psychic, isn't it?"

"*Psychic?*" He repeated the word as though he'd never heard it before.

"Some kind of energy within your planet fills you with power that you can control with your thoughts—in this case, healing power." She stopped and grinned at him. "That's just cool."

"Cool?"

"An expression from the Rock. Sorry."

Thane turned to the accoutrements spread out on the table. "I don't understand you, or any of this. But you cured Reana."

"You did too. Taking an anti-radiation dose can hurt like hell, but you took away the pain. I imagine that you'll be able to heal her the rest of the way now that the radiation sickness isn't eating her up inside."

"And others who have fallen ill will fare better once this thing is found and destroyed?"

"It will likely stop the Warding from degenerating too, although whether it can restore itself, I don't know."

"If the Warding is restored, no more ships can fall from the sky." Thane fixed his dark gaze on her. "And you cannot leave."

"I know."

She thought of the tight-beam signal she'd managed to send off to Justin before Thane had smashed the device. If Justin received it, he'd be on his way to find her. If the Warding failed completely, he could pinpoint her and take her home, but then the Four-One-Six Empire would find Pamaar.

But if the Warding was restored before Justin found her, Lea would be stuck here. Her own ship was far beyond repair and she had no fuel power it in any case.

She said slowly, "Every scout knows when they leave for a mission that they might not come back. We don't have families or anyone who will miss us. Our fellow scouts will hold a memorial ceremony for us and then get on with things. We ask one other scout to handle our legal affairs if we're lost and that's it."

Thane brushed her cheek with the backs of his fingers. "I cannot believe you aren't precious to someone."

"My mother and father are dead and I never married. I joined the scout unit when I was fresh out of flight school. We live to protect our home."

Loneliness welled up inside her as she spoke the words. She'd always been proud to think she'd sacrifice all for her people, but she realized she hadn't much to sacrifice. Or at least, not much to lose.

"You have me now," Thane said, as though reading her thoughts.

His eyes held so much darkness. He traced her lips with his thumb, powerful hands gentled for her.

"You're stuck with me, you mean." Lea tried to summon a smile. "If you don't want the other clans to claim me, you get the care and feeding of me."

He kissed the corner of her mouth, his breath hot. "Marry me, Lea."

Lea jumped. "Excuse me?"

"Bind with me. Become my wife." He touched her lips again. "Do you not have this kind of thing where you come from?"

"We do, but…" Confusion, happiness and sorrow burned in her chest, one emotion following swiftly after the other. "Why do you want to marry me?"

146

"Because, foolishly, I'm falling in love." His lips grazed her cheek. "Did you not notice?"

Justin always said there wasn't a situation in which Lea couldn't find words to express an opinion. Too bad Justin wasn't here to see her rendered speechless for the first time.

An ironic glint entered Thane's eyes. "I do not know if I can make you love me back. I do not know if I can make living here, away from all you know, bearable."

Dear goddess. Thane, leader of the lion-star clan, king of Pamaar, was worried that he couldn't make her happy. The number of men in Lea's life who had wanted to make her happy was exactly zero.

And he did make her happy—deliriously, dangerously happy. If she let herself, she'd be perfectly fine with abandoning her old life, settling down on beautiful Pamaar, letting Justin and everyone else on the Rock get along without her. Sorely tempting, especially since she might not be able to ever leave this place anyway.

"Isn't your life complicated enough already?" she asked him.

His smile was grim. "I do not consider you a complication. But I will leave the question to you while we will solve the problems of Felin and the Warding. Then, perhaps, I will be able to present Pamaar with a new queen."

Chapter Eleven
Search

ഔ

"He means it," Deon said.

He watched Lea flush as she stood next to him in her leather tunic, ready for flying, and remembered how sweet she looked all sexed and sleepy the night before.

"He's lost his mind," Lea said. "Felin has Challenged him to a duel to the death and radiation is killing his people, so he decides to plan a wedding."

"It will be wedding never to be forgotten." Deon grinned at her. "Troubadours will make songs of it, how the halls flowed with wine and the palace was drowned in flowers. The bride beautiful in violet and gold leading the king to his bedchamber, with the faithful Deon in tow. We'll make a lovely threesome."

"You want me to accept," she said, looking amazed.

They stood near the drake pens, Deon having sent a servant to fetch Cutie. Cutie snarled and pulled at his harness as he was led to them, showing off as usual, and Lea took a step back.

It always amused Deon how frightened Lea was of the drakes. She who'd come from beyond the Warding, who'd fallen from the sky and damn near died of it, who'd stood up to Felin and told him to kiss her ass was afraid of Cutie.

He helped her mount, suppressing a grin at her nervousness, and swung up behind her.

"Of course I want you to accept," he said as they launched skyward. "Thane's been unhappy for a long time— he tries to hide it, but I know. All of the sudden he's smiling again, ready to face Felin and win. He's stopped asking me if I'll run him through if necessary—all since you got here. So yes, I want him to marry you. Besides." He leaned around her and kissed her cheek. "I like you too."

She blushed again.

What a woman, Deon thought.

He chuckled as he pushed the drake higher, the beast fanning his leathery wings to soar on the thermals. Cutie loved to fly—he just liked making a big fuss about it.

Deon's task today was to take Lea over the landscape near Felin's territory to see if she could spot whatever she thought was causing the sickness. They flew in tight formation with five other drakes, Lea and Deon in the middle for maximum protection.

He didn't understand half of what she'd explained about the sickness, but he didn't need to understand. If Lea could help, he'd take her anywhere she wanted. Plus he planned to convince her to marry Thane. She was jumpy, like Cutie, worried about little things and facing big things without flinching.

She wanted to go home, sure, but why couldn't her home be here? There was nothing wrong with Pamaar. Even a soldier like himself could revel in the beauty of the place. Besides, Thane was here and who'd want to be without him?

"Where does the falcon-sword clan territory start?" she asked him over the wind.

Deon pointed to a low ridge of hills about a mile away. "Just beyond those. They'll be out patrolling their boundaries, you'd better believe."

"Why did Thane accept Felin's Challenge?"

"He had to, love. But he'll win. If you cure him, he'll win."

She looked glum. "You have a lot of faith in me."

"I didn't believe the seer at first. But you came here for a reason—a good reason—and I'm making sure you stay here until Thane is better."

Lea didn't answer, but that didn't bother Deon. He'd see to it that Thane won in the end, because the alternative didn't bear thinking about.

"We have to search inside Felin's territory," Lea said. "That's the most likely place. Thane told me his wife had gone to a village about twenty miles north of the city of the falcon-sword clan, and that's where she got sick. So it must be somewhere around there."

"Way too deep in Felin's territory. Too dangerous."

"I don't think we have a choice. If we go alone we have less chance of being spotted. How about if the rest of the phalanx noses around a little south of here while we skim west below the ridgeline? We can circle the city and come up on it from the side farthest from the lion-star territory."

Deon rumbled a laugh. "You've done this before."

"I was a scout. It was my job. I admit I've never done it on a scaly lizard that flies, but the concept is the same. I have the feeling you can steer Cutie as tight as I ever could my one-man craft."

"You got that right."

Deon swirled his arm in the air and signaled for the formation to land. He gave orders, then they were airborne again. Under cover of a thick, tree-lined hill, the other five drakes formed up and flew south while Deon waited, letting Cutie rest.

They did it as Lea described, skulking along the ridgeline then plunging into Felin's territory in deep shadow. Lea remained silent as they flew only a few feet above the ground, high enough for Cutie's wingspan to function but no higher. The drake stopped being grumpy and enjoyed himself—he liked covert operations.

The territory of the falcon-sword clan covered rocky miles that softened to meadow-covered hills with snow-capped mountains in the distance. A lovely place, if you weren't lucky enough to be lion-star.

Cutie flew low, far west and north of the city, which loomed as a sparkling white smudge on the distance. Felin was far away, camping out at the falcon-sword/lion-star border, ready to march on Thane at a moment's notice. Deon imagined that the city was busy preparing for the anticipated change in kingship, when the falcon-sword territory would control the government and Felin would take over Pamaar.

Not if I can help it, Deon promised silently.

They circled and searched, Lea looking for the gods knew what. Deon let Cutie fly as low as he liked while Lea hung from the saddle, no longer afraid, and searched the ground.

Shadows lengthened as the sun set—they'd have to find a place to spend the night soon.

The sun glinted off something in the distance, the spark of it slicing into his eyes, but when he turned to look, it had vanished. Deon wheeled the drake to investigate, but they found nothing before the sun disappeared behind the hills and twilight filled the sky.

"Damn, I'd give anything for my micro-binocs," Lea said. "The infra-red ones. We could search all night."

"I'm not even going to ask what those are. But Cutie can't search all night. He needs his beauty sleep."

Lea nodded. "Even scout ships need to dock for refueling."

Deon landed in a dense patch of forest with a clearing large enough for the drake. Drakes took off almost vertically, so they didn't need much room for that, only enough for Cutie to be able to curl up and snore.

He risked building a tiny fire so they wouldn't get too cold. He'd brought blankets that folded into compact bundles but which were finely woven and warm. He and Lea nibbled

151

soldier's rations, which were tasteless but would keep them going.

Lea grinned at him as he sat down next to her. "You're good at this."

"It's my job," Deon repeated her words. He slid his arm around her, pulled her close. "Let's see if we can figure out how to keep warm."

He kissed her for a while, liking the taste of her, reminding himself what it had felt like to have her mouth on him. Her sucking him while Thane pumped her. *Mmm, yes.*

If he'd been less worried about discovery by Felin's patrollers, he'd enjoy himself fucking tonight. As it was, he only allowed himself the pleasure of unlacing her leather top and licking the warm place between her breasts.

She hummed in enjoyment. "I don't think I'll ever get used to two men at the same time."

"Darling, you haven't *had* two men at the same time. I guarantee we'll make you dance with pleasure."

"You're sure about that, are you?"

He loved the teasing twinkle in her green eyes. Who knew that a falling star would contain such a wonderful woman?

"You'll love every second of it, I promise."

"I'll hold you to that."

He loved her breasts, the firm roundness that fit into his hands, her skin creamy soft against his work-rough fingers. He sucked one taut nipple into his mouth while she continued to make noises of pleasure.

He enjoyed licking her for a while, then regretfully made himself sit up and simply hold her. They were too far into Felin's territory to risk not staying alert.

At least he could wrap his arms around her and let her blonde-and-brown hair tickle his nose. Pleasure didn't *all* have to be fucking—although nothing beat fucking.

She rested her head on his shoulder, content. "So how did you and Thane meet?"

Ah, memories. But maybe telling the story would distract Deon from how horny he was.

"My father was weapons-maker for the clan leader, who was Thane's father at the time. We lived above the forge on the edge of the palace grounds, not too near, you understand, so the smoky smell didn't get into the pristine palace. The tiger-vessel clan ruled at the time and Thane's father was next in line for kingship."

"And you and Thane became friends?"

Deon chuckled, remembering. "Not right away. I thought he was a snotty rich kid, too soft to get his hands dirty doing real work. I used to taunt him something awful—softly, so my father wouldn't hear and wale on me. Thane heard, though. I kept expecting him to have his guards come down and teach me a lesson, but they never did. So one day I sneered that he was a coward and he turned around and started pummeling me."

Lea's eyes widened. "How old were you?"

"Seven or eight, I think. I had to admit that the rich kid could pack a punch. We fought pretty hard and by the time my father and his guards pulled us apart, he was as muddy and dirty and beat up as me.

"My father gave me the *he's going to be clan-leader someday, maybe even king* lecture, but I didn't care. I started to lay in wait for him and he'd ditch his guards and we'd fight almost every day. He told me later that he was anxious to prove he was just as tough as a smithy's son."

"Did he ever win?"

Deon shook his head. "It was usually a draw. I had strength from working the forge, but he was trained in arms by the best soldiers. He knew elegant tricks and I just knew how to fight dirty. We started teaching each other."

"Male bonding," she murmured.

"We became best friends, if that's what you mean. If you mean lovers, we didn't until we were about twenty and I was ready to go off to learn to be a soldier for real. I wanted to be in the palace guard, because by that time Thane's da' had died and now Thane was clan leader.

"I wanted to learn to protect Thane, so I left for training. The night he came to see me off, we both realized we wouldn't meet up again for a year. That's when we knew. We'd played with courtesans together after our coming of age at eighteen, but never with each other. It was quite a night."

"I'll bet," Lea said.

"And then, while I was training, the tiger-vessel leader died of old age and Thane was king of Pamaar. When I came back, Thane requested me to be his personal bodyguard and his lover and I accepted. We sacred-bonded seven years after that."

Lea looked thoughtful. "From what Thane explained, if you weren't his personal bodyguard, you could be his lover more — um — deeply."

"I could fuck *him*, you mean?" He tasted faint regret, as usual. "That's true, but then, I might not be there when he needed me. Like this, I can take care of him, protect him. No one goes near him without my say-so. I'll sacrifice the beauty of having my cock inside him to keep him whole and alive. I love him enough to keep my frustrations under control."

"That's sweet," Lea said.

"Sweet?" Deon snorted. "It's necessary. Don't think it's easy for me. Or him. The mush-hearted git refuses to have any other lover in him because law says he can't have me. It's his way."

"But I thought Balin..."

"Balin has been cleared to screw the king, if Thane wants it, but he's never asked for it. He says it's me or no one." He narrowed his eyes. "Are you going to say that's *sweet* too?"

"Yes."

"Yuck. Thane and I should just relieve ourselves with courtesans and get over it. This noble sacrifice stuff is cloying."

Lea's smile was knowing. "So why don't you?"

He sobered, every emotion he felt for Thane swimming to the surface. "It wouldn't be the same."

"There should be a ballad about you two."

He growled. "Don't even think about it. Now, what do I have to do to wipe that smile off your face? Hmm, let me think."

She kept smiling, though, and laughing as he kissed her and slid his hands into the leggings he loosened with quick fingers.

"Don't make too much noise, love," he murmured into her ear. "We have to be silent out here."

"You're evil," she whispered.

"You kept calling me *sweet*. Payback is a bitch."

She muffled her laugh and then her groan of delight as he found the place that made her squirm. His cock was rock-hard from their conversation and her delightful body, and he was going to make her pay.

In the darkness, Cutie moved, his *there's-something-out-there* fidget. Deon suppressed a growl of frustration as he looked up and reached for his sword. Couldn't Felin's people have waited a *little* longer?

Lea had heard the faint sounds as well, her soldier's hearing almost as good as his. She nodded when he silently signaled for her to stay put.

He adjusted his leggings over his rapidly deflating cock, wrapped his hand securely around the sword and melted into the darkness.

Lea, bless her heart, stayed where she was, utterly silent. Cutie did his best to look like a statue—although why there'd be a statue of a drake way out here, Deon couldn't say. But the drake would come to his aid if necessary.

155

Deon crept through the dark woods, moving slowly enough to not blunder into anything but fast enough to cover ground. He saw an upright shadow that wasn't a tree just as Cutie turned his head and growled.

Deon heard the intruder shout in surprise and fear, then an explosion rang in his ears and hot smoke filled his lungs. He'd smelled that acrid odor only once before, when Lea's strange weapon had split a boulder in two.

He plunged forward. Lea was on her feet in the clearing, facing a tall man who held a weapon that looked just like hers. Cutie snarled and snapped and spit irritable streams of fire.

Deon sprang onto the man from behind, wrapped one arm around him and pressed his trusty blade to the intruder's throat.

"Surprise," Deon said in a cold voice. "But not as surprised as Felin will be when I send you back in pieces."

"No!" Lea had her hands up, her eyes wide. "Deon, wait. Don't hurt him. I know him. It's Justin, my friend from the Rock."

* * * * *

"What the hell is going on?" Justin demanded of Lea. "Who *is* this guy?"

He sat cross-legged on the blankets in his flight suit, Lea next to him. Deon stood over them, a hulking wall of muscle, insisting on keeping his sword trained on Justin.

"He's Lord Deon, personal bodyguard to the king of Pamaar."

"King of where?" Justin blinked. "There's no such place. This planet doesn't even show up on any of the charts."

"Yes I know. They have a shield—it's a long story."

Justin glanced up at Deon. "I have the feeling he doesn't have the patience for long stories. Do you, big fella?"

"He can't understand you. But he understands me, so watch it."

"How can that be? You're speaking our language, not his."

Lea waved away explanations. "It's a psychic thing, which the king... Never mind. We really don't have time for this, or to even ask how you found me. Do you have your ship? Did you see anything when you came down, like a wreck or something else giving off a ton of radiation?"

"I was homing in on you." Justin tapped her skull behind her ear, where Lea's implant was.

Deon didn't like him touching her. He slid the sword in front of Justin's face and gave him a warning smile.

Justin's hazel eyes widened. "Goddess, are they all big bad barbarians like him?"

"No, they're all strong, but some of them have quite good manners." She shot Deon a glare.

Deon grunted like an ancient caveman. "I only understand half your conversation, but I get it. Tell him that under different circumstances, I'd think he was cute."

"What?" Justin demanded. "I see your face, Lea. What did he say?"

"He said he thinks you're cute."

Justin gulped. Lea had always thought her friend handsome, with his light brown hair, hazel eyes and a tall, lean body that his skin-tight flight suit outlined well. Deon, grinning, obviously did too.

"Holy goddess," Justin breathed.

Deon lowered his sword so that the tip grazed Justin's nose. "Or I could split him in two."

Justin eyed the sword point. "I don't think I need that translated."

"Deon, stop it," Lea said. "Justin can help us, so stop being a bully-boy."

"But I *am* a bully-boy."

"He isn't going to hurt me."

Deon moved the tip from Justin's face but didn't sheath the weapon. "We don't know if Felin got to him first."

"True." She bit her lip.

"What?" Justin asked in alarm. "I don't like the way you're looking at me."

"I'm wondering how long you've been here, where you landed, who you met and how you found me."

Justin looked puzzled. "Two standard hours, about eight kilometers from here, I didn't meet anyone until I saw that dragon-thing and I tracked you." Justin waved at the device resting on the blanket beside Lea, designed to home in on a fallen scout's implant.

Lea repeated this to Deon, who shrugged. "He could be telling the truth, or he might not be," Deon said. "I can torture him a little, if you want."

Lea had still not entirely caught on to when Deon teased and when he was serious. "Leave him alone. We can use his ship to help us."

"Or we can use my ship to get out of here," Justin looked her up and down, from her mussed and dusty hair to the Pamaaran leather tunic and leggings she'd donned for the ride. "You and me, kid. You know there's room for me to take a scout in trouble and I'd say you were a scout in trouble."

"It's more complicated than that."

"Why? Have you been brainwashed by the locals?" Justin forced his expression to remain neutral under Deon's watchful stare. "You have my gun. You can stun him and probably even that big beast and then we blast off this ball before he wakes up."

Lea glanced at Deon. She remembered trying to stun Felin when he'd first found her and how the big man had barely staggered when the beam hit him. She'd have to heavily stun

Deon before he went down, a setting which might even kill him. She had the feeling Cutie wouldn't be felled easily, either. The people of Pamaar were tough.

Justin understood. He and Lea knew each other well enough that they could execute a plan without speaking. Only this time Lea couldn't simply cut and run.

"I'm helping them find a source of radiation, something unshielded, that's killing them. They saved me and healed me when I crashed and I owe it to them."

Justin made a conceding gesture. "All right. I can see that. Will they let you go when you're done?"

Lea thought of Thane, his warm smile and the heat in his eyes when he'd asked her to marry him. She shrugged, not trusting herself to speak.

"I get it," Justin said. "We'll talk about it later. If this is legit, sure, use my ship. But would you tell this guy to back off? I can't tell whether he wants to kill me or screw me."

"Don't worry," Lea said, climbing to her feet. "He's in love with someone else." She patted Deon's broad bicep, right over the snarling lion.

"Hey," Deon growled, swatting her on the butt. "Don't ruin my fun."

Chapter Twelve
Revelations

ஐ

Justin's ship was exactly eight kilometers away, as he'd said, and a little east of their camp. Lea remembered how Deon had seen a brief glint of metal in the setting sun and decided it must have been Justin landing.

Lea took over the scout ship, telling Justin to fly drakeback with Deon. She gave Justin his helmet, which he'd left locked behind the pilot's seat—she could broadcast to it using the ship's controls while he rode with Deon.

Justin wasn't happy she wanted him to stay with Deon, but she told him to lump it. "He won't let you alone with me and he's too big to fit in the ship with us. I know what I'm looking for and with your scanners I can find it fast, even in the dark. Deon won't hurt you." She hesitated. "Will you, Deon?"

Deon curled his lip and looked threatening. He was a fearsome sight, with his tattoos and sword, his blue-beaded braids and his thick leather.

"Stop that," Lea said grumpily. She hopped into the cockpit of the ship, liking the familiar feeling of her butt sinking into the pilot's seat, the steering shaft nestling between her legs.

"I'll wait until Cutie is away," she said, clicking the preliminary switches. "I don't want to scare him."

"Good thinking." Deon leaned down, seized her face between his hands and gave her a rough, hot kiss.

Lea thought she loved him at that moment. He was trusting her to use forbidden technology he didn't understand to help his people, and trusting her not to simply fly away from Pamaar in Justin's ship. He was willing to take her at her word and that warmed her because she knew Deon didn't trust lightly. He would be in as much trouble as she was if the ship was discovered, and he was willing to take the risk.

"Take care of Justin," she said. "He's a good friend."

"Right." Deon winked, then shot out his hand and grabbed Justin's ass.

Justin jumped, flushing. "You'd better know what you're doing," he muttered at Lea. But he jammed on his helmet and followed Deon to the waiting Cutie.

As soon as the drake launched into the sky, Lea finished her engine checks and fired it up. She didn't worry about noise because scout ships were meant to operate with a minimum of sound. How could a person sneak around and scout if her ship sounded like the latest racing model?

It felt so good to fly again. Lea's heart swelled until it hurt, knowing she was born for this life and realizing how much she missed it.

If she accepted Thane's offer, she could never fly again. But if she left with Justin, she'd never see Thane again and that would be that.

She wiped an annoying tear from her cheek and let the ship glide into the air. Choices would have to be made later, the feelings in her heart saved for another time. That's what scouts did, put the job before their personal life.

She'd always thought that sucked.

Lea felt funny flying without helmet and flight suit, her leather garb made for drake-flight, not the precision fit of the cockpit. She had to wiggle around before she could get comfortable, then she flicked on the console mic and tapped it.

"Can you hear me, Justin?"

"Yes," Justin's voice crackled. "Hey, this drake thing is fun."

"Figures you'd like it. Anyway, keep tracking me. I'm going for a pass near the city."

"Be careful," Justin said, heartfelt.

"Always am."

Lea guided the ship over the rolling terrain, the night-sights on the console picking up every curve. In the distance the city of the falcon-sword clan showed up as a green blur.

Every nerve tingled as she flew, the ship dodging and skimming to her slightest touch. The feeling of being one with the craft was exhilarating and she realized she'd missed it more than she'd thought.

With all the stealth equipment and multi-layered tracking devices packed into Justin's ship, it didn't take her long to find what she was looking for. She saw it in the ground first, the faint yellowish tint on the instruments that warned of radiation.

She skimmed over a hill and there it was, half-buried at the bottom of a bowl-like valley, a bright yellow blotch on her readouts, though in reality, it was only a dark smudge in deep shadow.

The readouts meant, *Radiation at dangerous levels.*

Lea took the nose up so she wouldn't pass too close to the source of radiation, though the plating of the hull protected her. She took a series of images as she flew over once, twice, three times.

"Justin, I'm feeding you what I've found. Can you see that?"

"Yep." Justin sounded grim. "What is it?"

"I'm not sure. I'll have to look more closely at the images when I land. It's about one hundred kilometers north and west of the falcon-clan's city. I'm coming back."

Static crackled and Deon's voice came to her. "How can I hear you when you're so far away?"

"Magic, Deon."

"Bullshit. Just get back here in one piece. I don't trust all this *technology*."

Lea laughed at him and angled the craft to follow the warm green blip that was Cutie and his passengers.

* * * * *

Lea landed the craft well inside lion-star territory and she and Justin and Deon hid it with branches and rock and mud. She mounted the drake in front of Justin, and Deon headed them back to Thane's city.

Justin patted Cutie's shoulder as they flew. "I wonder how fast one of these can go. I bet you can get some good acrobatic flying on them."

"They're called drakes," Lea said. "And they're alive, with sharp teeth."

Justin gave her a puzzled look. "If they were that dangerous no one would be able to ride them. This guy's like my dad's horses back home — they had lots of attitude, but they liked when I rode them flat out. I won races and everything."

"I'm sure you and Deon can have a nice chat about them."

"I'm looking forward to it," Deon rumbled, giving Justin a leer.

Justin flinched. "Make him stop that."

Lea couldn't help laughing and Deon joined in.

They landed in the courtyard of the palace, guards flowing out to meet them, headed by Thane. While Justin expressed awe at the intricate architecture of the palace, Lea slid from the drake into Thane's arms.

He held her close, his wool tunic and cloak as soft and warm as his kiss. "Welcome home," he said.

Lea returned the kiss, letting Thane's warmth and scent flow over her like summer air.

She parted from him to find Justin at her shoulder, his mouth open in shock. "But I thought you and Deon..." He glanced back at Deon, who was delivering Cutie to his handler.

Lea took Thane's hand, resisting the urge to kiss it. "Thane, this is Justin. Is there somewhere we can talk?"

Thane understood that she couldn't reveal all she found, including Justin, in front of the full courtyard. Not only were guards there, but every servant had seemed to find an excuse to be passing through—washerwomen, smiths, drake-handlers, harness makers, maids and even the attendant who'd shown Lea the library.

Thane led her and Justin through the crowd to the palace, still holding Lea's hand. A woman had come to join the throng, her dark hair falling like sable satin to her knees. Justin gaped when he looked at her and the woman gave him a sultry smile.

"Who is *that?*" Justin breathed, head swiveling to keep her in sight.

Lea had seen the interlaced tattoos on the underside of her arms. "She's a courtesan. They're very upper-class here, considered artists in the ways of pleasure."

"Good attitude." He kept looking at her until Lea thought his neck would snap. Deon laughed and rumbled something behind him.

"Deon says he'll introduce you if you want."

Justin brightened. "Can he? I think I'm beginning to like him."

Deon and Justin, both soldiers, both fascinated by flying things and both liking beautiful women. They'd get along all right.

Thane ordered everyone out of his private sitting room, Deon having to assure the reluctant guards that he'd keep a sharp eye on Justin. Lea had already heard the comments that Justin had no tattoos on his face and wore strange garb, coupled with speculative glances at Lea, also tattooless as far as they knew.

As soon as the door closed, Thane reached for Lea. "Come here."

He held her close, then kissed her again, his arms tight around her. Deon stepped next to them, his fingers skimming her spine and Thane's.

"Lea," Justin said with laughter in his voice. "You slut, you."

Thane took his time finishing the kiss and when he eased away, Deon brushed the side of her mouth with his lips.

But as Thane straightened up and moved his attention to Justin, he was every inch the king. His hard gaze was piercing, a man sizing up an intruder who might signal disaster for his kingdom.

Justin winced when Thane touched his head, but Lea said, "It's all right. Let him."

Thane closed his eyes and by now Lea knew he was learning Justin, seeing the patterns that made up his aura.

Thane opened his eyes and lowered his hand. "Do you understand me?"

Justin looked startled. "Yes. How did he do that? Lea, where the fuck am I?"

Thane turned to Lea. "He came from beyond the Warding, in response to the signal you sent when we went out to your ship?"

"I'm afraid so."

Thane's eyes were bleak. "He found you and came here, despite the Warding. Which can only mean it has weakened to the point that we are open to others from beyond it."

"Unless we can fix it," Lea said quickly. "Let me show you what I found."

She'd brought the holo-projector from Justin's ship, a tiny device which she now set on the polished wooden table. She touched it and a series of three-dimensional images began slowly rotating through the air.

Deon leaned forward, fascinated, though Thane watched with more caution.

Justin squinted at the pictures. "Looks like pieces of a probe."

"One that blew up before it hit atmosphere," Lea said, assessing the images with a scout's practiced eye.

The remains looked like lumps of metal or polished rock half buried in hard dirt and covered with vegetation. Anyone could walk by them without noticing—they glowed yellow through the scout ship's instruments and in the holo-photos but would look like ordinary rock in daylight.

"Likely Four-One-Six Empire," she concluded.

Deon tentatively put a finger to the holo-image, his tattooed forehead moving with amazement as his fingertip went right through it.

Justin touched the projector to zoom and sharpen a corner of one picture, which showed a few much-battered symbols. "It's from the empire all right. But an old model. Nothing they use now. Must have crashed years ago, maybe decades."

"What does this mean?" Thane broke in. "That something from this empire you speak of came through the Warding long ago? How?"

Justin looked at Lea. "Theory is your area, babe. I just fly low and get the dirt."

Lea nodded, feeling elated and depressed at the same time. Elated because she thought she knew the answer and depressed because it wasn't a good answer.

"What I *think* happened," she began, "is that a probe exploded above Pamaar a long time ago, maybe because it was faulty or maybe the Warding interfered with it—who knows? A chunk of the probe was so irradiated that it weakened the Warding enough to slip through and fall to the planet. It was in such a remote area that no one noticed, or if they saw it, they thought it was a piece of asteroid—a falling star."

"And it's lain there ever since?" Thane asked.

"Looks like it. No one's disturbed the site, no one's noticed it."

"But it's glowing." Deon pointed at the image. "How could we not notice that?"

Lea touched the projector, removing the overlay of instrument readings. The glow faded and the probe again resembled lumps of rock in the dark. "Because that's what it really looks like."

Deon stared a while longer. "Huh."

"And this is why the Warding is weak and my people are dying?" Thane asked skeptically.

"I'm pretty sure. Once the probe's shields broke down all the way, the radiation got into your planet and weakened part of the Warding—which is connected to Pamaar in a bizarre way that's not just physical. The damaged Warding weakened your binding to it, which made you not able to heal the people who had fallen ill from radiation sickness. Kind of a vicious circle."

Thane went silent, staring at the innocent-looking lumps of metal that were destroying his planet.

Deon rested his large fists on the table. "And the weak Warding let Justin find you. Which means more people from beyond the Warding can come after *him*."

Lea nodded. "Including the Four-One-Six Empire."

Deon turned a furious stare on Justin.

"Hey, no one tracked my ship," Justin said swiftly. "I know how to go after a fallen scout without the empire knowing about it. And no way was I going to ignore a distress call from Lea."

"I trust *you* to cover your tracks," Lea said, more for Thane's and Deon's benefit. "But the Warding is a baffler shield. If it continues to deteriorate, this planet will start showing up on scanners and the empire will find it."

"And *harvest* us," Deon said. "That's the word you used."

"Yes."

Justin studied the delicate archways of the room, the gilded and carved wooden furniture, the view of the soaring hills and sky outside the floor-to-ceiling windows. "That would suck."

"Which is why we're going to fix it." Lea turned a hard look on her best friend and comrade in arms. "You and me, Justin."

Justin thought a moment, then shrugged. "Why not? I'm all for screwing the empire."

"Not just the empire. Everyone. No one must know of Pamaar—not the Rock, not any of the other independents, no one."

"I get it."

Lea fell silent, wondering if he really did get it.

Thane watched Justin thoughtfully then turned an even more speculative gaze on Lea. "How do you suggest we repair the Warding? I don't even know if that's possible." His dark gaze flicked back to the images. "We can destroy this."

"That might not do any good," Lea countered. "We can shield it, using pieces of the hull of my ship, which is built to withstand a ton of radiation, or we can break it into smaller pieces and carry it, shielded, to various parts of Pamaar—so each area has a tiny amount, not a concentrated dose. The radiation will fade eventually, but by eventually, I mean decades, maybe centuries."

"This is something I can arrange," Deon said. "The only trouble is, this *probe* as you call it is deep inside Felin's territory."

"I'll have to tell him." Thane kept his eyes on the image, his voice somber. "It's his people the probe is killing first. He deserves to know."

"He'll think it's a trick," Deon warned.

"We will have to convince him, then." He glanced once at Deon and his jaw hardened. "I want Justin and this device well-guarded, Lea also. And I need a meeting with Felin — alone. No guards, no entourage. Felin can bring a trusted bodyguard, but I will have only you and Lea."

Deon scowled. "I don't like that idea."

"I know you don't, but it must be done. Felin isn't stupid — he will understand the implications."

Lea stood up, heart speeding with hope. "Do you think, if he knows what's going on and that you can fix it, that he'll withdraw The Challenge?"

Thane shook his head. "The Challenge cannot be withdrawn. Once issued, it must be seen through to the end."

"Don't tell me — it's the law." Lea sighed. "I wish you didn't have so many laws."

Thane's lips quirked. "It allows us to live well. But don't worry, Lea. I intend to win."

* * * * *

Felin read the message from Thane while the two lion-and-pentacle tattooed men waited uneasily just inside his tent.

I've discovered what is killing our people, Thane had written. *It is a device from beyond the Warding and if we shield it, the Warding will be restored and men and women will stop dying. Let us meet as clan leaders and invite the leaders of our fellow clans, dragon-wand and tiger-vessel, and discuss how we will stop this. I do not seek to sidestep the Challenge, which will be met, but we should put it off until the Warding can be restored. The health of our people is more important than our personal battle.*

Oh, well spoken, Felin thought grimly. *As though the Challenge is for my personal gain and not to stop falcon-sword people from dying. Arrogant bastard.*

He dismissed the messengers and most of his own staff, then left his tent and walked out in the gathering darkness. Dusky hills rolled to the horizon, beautiful and green, his beloved Pamaar.

Never in Pamaar's recorded history had the Warding been so weak. The binding between Warding and king sometimes didn't work well, but the Warding itself had always been strong.

He touched the bloodstone around his neck and couldn't help smiling. He wondered what the reaction of Thane and his fuck-partner Deon had been when they saw the falcon tattoo spread in all its glory across Lea's hip. Felin knew damn well he'd broken the rules having her tattooed while she was unconscious, but it was worth it.

He remembered Lea's tight little ass upended so the tattoo artist could work. She was a lovely, lush female that he wouldn't mind having in his bed. He'd stick a sword through Thane and take Lea as his queen, thus fulfilling the ridiculous prophecy and winning the faith of Pamaarans everywhere.

If she let him into her bed, well and good, or she could have courtesans, as she liked. He wanted to save his world, not go for a sexual conquest.

Felin had no doubt he could win the Challenge. Thane had weakened considerably and Felin possessed the bloodstone of the queen from the sky. His cause was sacred and he knew it.

"My lord." Rasheed, his trusted guard with the blue-whorl tattoos on his face approached. "Lord Thane's messengers grow impatient for your reply."

"Lion-stars are too soft. What they mean is they don't want to spend the night in a camp, but want to get home to their warm, cushy beds. Bring me pen and paper; I'll write my reply."

Rasheed bowed. "My lord."

That was one thing about Rasheed Felin liked — the man didn't talk too much.

As Rasheed beat a retreat, Felin lifted the bloodstone from around his neck. The movement pushed open his loose leather vest and he looked regretfully down at the lesions that had begun to form on his broad chest of late — the same kind Lady Cerena and Emilie's daughter had showed.

He would kill Thane, heal the land and then heal his people, himself last. He closed his hand around the bloodstone and began to walk back to his tent.

* * * * *

Deon read the message Thane showed him in disgust.

When the Challenge is met, Felin had written, *I will speak to you.*

"Idiot," Deon said, rage boiling through him. He and Thane had been alone when the second message came, Lea asleep after their tiring flight, Justin eating and resting in a guarded room. "He could save his clan, be a hero."

"He doesn't trust us," Thane answered. "Were I in his place, I might do the same. Send back a message that I will meet his Challenge, tomorrow, in the plain by the Warding caves."

"Tomorrow?" Deon repeated incredulously.

"The sooner we get this finished the sooner we can start shielding that thing, as Lea suggests, and I can start the healing. I will prepare tonight and fight tomorrow."

Deon regarded him for a long time, his face clouded. "You're the king," he finally conceded.

"I am. At least until we go to the place of the Challenge."

"Thane."

Thane put his hand on Deon's shoulders and kissed him lightly on the lips. "Look after Lea for me, whatever happens. She knows what to do, so you must keep her safe and make sure she can do it."

"You're going to win," Deon said stubbornly. "I won't let you lose."

"Either way, you have to promise me you'll protect Lea. Even if it means letting me die."

"Damn you."

"Promise me. I need to know I can count on you."

"So you can die without worry?" Deon demanded. "You really are a bastard, you know that?"

Thane cupped Deon's face in his strong hands. "Just promise me."

Deon's eyes moistened, to his irritation. "You know I'll kill anyone who gets near her."

"Good man. Strip for me now. We don't have much time, but I can still get in one good fuck before we go."

"Huh. You can never resist a quickie."

"Thank you," Thane said softly.

Deon started unlacing his leather tunic, turning away so Thane wouldn't see the tears running down his face.

Chapter Thirteen
Preparations

Preparing for the Challenge meant spending the night at the chosen place. In practical terms, Lea mused that evening as the drakes landed near the tents servants had traveled ahead to erect, the ritual made sense. The two fighters had a chance to rest from their journey and could emerge refreshed onto the place of battle in the morning.

Thane's tent was, as Lea expected, huge and opulent. Thick tapestries and silk hangings divided it into separate rooms for sleeping, bathing, eating and receiving guests. The bedroom was little more than a large expanse of cushions taking up the entire curtained off space.

Lea expected Thane to prepare by practicing sword thrusts with Deon or some such thing, but instead he spent the rest of the evening reading books and scrolls, signing papers and speaking with his councilors.

"Putting things right," Deon whispered to her through a crack in the silk hangings. She and Justin waited in the bedroom, out of sight, while Deon watched over Thane and communicated surreptitiously through the drapes. "In case."

Lea didn't want to think about "in case".

When the councilors retreated the servants served a lavish meal, which Thane did not eat. Challengers were supposed to fast, Thane said—Felin would be doing the same. Lea tried to eat but couldn't force much down.

Thane turned to Justin after the servants cleared the table, seeming to not have noticed everyone's lack of appetite. "Justin, you have been of help to me and a good friend to Lea. I wish to reward you."

Justin looked surprised and Thane snapped his fingers. On cue, the curtains to the sitting room parted and the brown-haired courtesan Justin had admired entered. She bowed to Thane, then turned a stunning smile on Justin.

"Is he kidding?" Justin turned an amazed look to Lea. He'd been a little crabby since Thane had locked away his pistol and other scout implements, though he'd kept his protests to himself. "You're kidding me, right?" he asked Thane.

"Panece was most interested when I sent word asking if she would be willing to come to you. She saw you yesterday and liked the look of you."

Justin flushed. "I guess you're not kidding."

Thane regarded him with the same ease he'd had when he'd first offered Lea the use of the best courtesans in the kingdom. "A tent has been prepared for you if you prefer privacy. Though you are welcome to stay here and join—"

Justin leapt to his feet. "No. No joining. I'll just... Um. I'll just talk to Panece in the other tent..."

"I'd go before you do any more stuttering," Lea said.

"Right." Justin glanced at each of them, then shrugged and sighed. "When in Rome..."

He got himself out of the tent but was gentlemanly enough to hold the tent flap open for Panece, who was trying not to laugh. Lea noted the guards that silently detached themselves to follow at a discreet distance.

"What's Rome?" Deon growled.

Lea grinned at him. "It's an ancient saying from an ancient civilization on an ancient world."

Deon dropped it. "You're trusting him," he told Thane.

"It doesn't matter." Thane rose and unlaced the gray outer tunic he wore. Beneath was a sleeveless tunic of dark blue silk. "He won't betray me on the eve of the Challenge. If he thinks to, the guards will explain the penalty."

"Penalty?" Lea asked.

"The penalty for betraying or hurting either competitor in the Challenge is instant death," Deon said.

She paled. "Harsh."

"No one would." Thane came to her and took her hands, raising her to her feet. "The law must be harsh, because tonight, in effect, Pamaar has no king." He smiled. "Besides, Panece will keep him occupied."

"You planned that."

Thane kissed the corner of Lea's mouth. "I did. I wanted him out of the way and busy so I could use the time to say goodbye."

Deon locked his hand around Thane's bicep. "What you mean to say is, *This time tomorrow I'll be king again, don't worry.*"

"You always worry, Deon."

"Someone has to," Deon growled.

* * * * *

Thane said goodbye by having Lea ride him. He stretched himself across the cushioned bed, his large body spread for her delight. He was deep inside her, feeling her tightness squeezing him, loving the way Lea let herself enjoy every second.

She kept her silk robe crumpled around her hips, hiding the falcon tattoo from him. He wanted to tell her he didn't mind—she could have it removed and a brilliant-colored lion in its place. He would watch the entire task and even lend a hand—clan leaders always learned tattoo art.

Deon knelt behind Lea, his legs on either side of hers, broad hands on her breasts. "Sweet," he breathed, nibbling on Lea's neck as her orgasm took her. "Too sweet."

"She's adorable," Thane agreed. He lay back, flushed and warm from his own release.

Lea was beautiful, her variegated blonde hair mussed, short curls sticking up every which way. He was perfectly happy she'd dropped into his life, no matter how strange the circumstances—the gods giving him a taste of joy among his troubles.

Now she smiled as Deon nuzzled her cheek, his hands on the curve of her waist.

"I'm loving all this attention," she said.

"Do you want more?" Thane offered. "I can send for Balin if you like."

"No." She leaned against Deon's shoulder. "I want it to be just us."

"No argument from me," Deon said.

Lea looked thoughtful as she stroked her nails across Thane's chest, back and forth, back and forth, barely scratching.

"You know," she said, "tonight, you are not the king."

Thane ran his fingertips across her moving hands. "No. I am merely a man called Thane. Can you forgive me?"

She smiled, as though amused by something. He suddenly caught on to what she was thinking and his gaze flicked to Deon.

Deon's eyes went slate black. "Don't tempt me."

Thane was rock-hard, never mind that he'd just had one of his best releases ever. "If I am not king tonight…"

"You will be again."

"Not if Felin kills me," Thane pointed out.

"I won't let him."

"You can not interfere with the Challenge," Thane said.

They looked at each other, eyes sparking, while Lea sat between them, a smug smile on her face.

"We have a saying on the Rock," Lea began.

"When in Rome?" Deon asked.

"No. *Go for it.* You might not be alive tomorrow."

Deon shook his head. "You come from a mysterious clan."

Thane grinned and stroked Lea's arm. "I like it. Very smart women in the Rock clan. Sexy too."

"So, are we going to talk all night?" Deon growled. "Or are you going to let me fuck you?"

Lea lay down at Thane's side. She was excited, her nipples dark with tension, her light jade eyes starry. He loved her—he'd do anything for her—and he loved Deon. This might be the best night of his life.

And his last.

"I want to watch this," Lea said, her chest rising with excited breaths.

"No," Thane said. "I want to be in you."

"Even better," Deon agreed. "You ready?"

"I've been ready for ten years."

Deon laughed as he rose from the cushions like a god of old. "You two get settled while I find out what kind of lube is in this well-stocked tent."

Thane shook with excitement as he rolled over onto Lea and she smiled at him, warm and welcoming.

This generous woman had been willing to risk so much to help his people, even though she had little to gain by it. She was far from home in a strange land and still she gave. She also sensed what Thane needed to be happy and she offered it without any thought of recompense.

In return, he determined to give her as much pleasure from it as he possibly could.

He looked down at her lovely face and brushed a kiss to her lips. "Open for me," he whispered.

She was already wet and swollen from their lovemaking and he easily slipped inside. He kept his gaze firmly on Lea, resisting the temptation to look over his shoulder to see what Deon did.

Deon hummed in his throat as he banged around in the chests and cupboards that had been brought so his every need would be served.

"This isn't a tent," he rumbled. "It's a frigging palace. Poor little rich king."

Thane closed his eyes and enjoyed being inside Lea, ignoring Deon.

"When I learned soldiering, we slept twenty men to a tiny canvas tent," Deon went on. "No cushions and silver washbasins and gold plates for us."

Lea moaned, clutching Thane's shoulders. Thane felt Deon kneel behind him and he slowed his thrusts.

Cool lube touched between his cheeks and then—*oh gods*—the pressure of Deon's finger. His entire body contracted in pleasure.

"Don't squeeze so hard," Deon growled.

"I can't help it."

"You need to be loose and light for me. I've got a huge cock—*ow.*"

Thane, excited, had squeezed hard again. "Stop talking, then."

"Don't pay attention to me." Deon sounded amused. "Focus on Lea."

Not a hard thing to do. Thane opened his eyes to see Lea watching with her jade-green gaze, her eyes so beautiful he could drown in them. He felt her closing around him and switched his attention to that point of pleasure.

"There you go." Deon played with him a little more, ringing him with fingers and thumb, sliding fingertips inside.

Thane concentrated on Lea and made his body relax to Deon's ministrations. He lost all track of time between the erotic feeling of Deon playing with him and the wild excitement of Lea under him. He heard Deon saying, *Almost there,* then a lot of lube and then the heat of Deon's body on his back.

Thane lifted his hips, staying inside Lea, who lifted herself to him. The pillows helped and for some reason their gold tassels and purple silk patterns caught and held his gaze.

And then Deon was sliding inside him, a huge, hard length, slick with lube. His friend, his partner, his lover for so long finally *in* him.

Deon's cock pressed all the way inside, slowly, slowly, widening him, opening him. The feeling of Deon's balls tight against his backside made him writhe and he loved the tickling of Deon's wiry hair on his skin.

"I love you," Deon told him. "I fucking love you." He traced the outlines of the lion on Thane's back. "You and your badass tattoos."

Under Thane, Lea went over the edge. She cried out, hips moving against his. His excitement exploded but he didn't want to release, not yet. Deon was pumping now, groaning, his strong hands firm on Thane's back.

"I can't stand it," Thane whispered.

"Yes you can. You can take me. You're damn strong, you always have been, even when you were beating me up when we were eight."

"The smithy's son with the gorgeous eyes. I wanted to fight and fight so I'd stop wanting to kiss you."

"Didn't work. I'm irresistible."

"You fuck good. I love you fucking me."

"You betcha." Deon groaned. "*Gods,* no, I'm not ready yet."

His scalding seed flooded inside Thane, a sensation Thane had wanted forever.

Deon landed on Thane's back, breathing hard. They lay in an exhausted pile, all three of them breathing hard, sweat coating their skin. Under Thane, Lea gave a tired laugh.

"This is fun."

Thane kissed her. "You aren't wrong about that."

Deon rumbled and growled, at last sliding off Thane's back to land full-length on the cushions next to them. He wiped the sweat from his face.

"Did you like that?"

Thane leaned over and kissed him full on the mouth. "You know damn well I did."

Deon's eyes sparkled. "In that case." He rubbed his hands and his grin widened. "You ain't seen nothing yet."

* * * * *

The Challenge began as soon as it was light.

Thane wore leather greaves on his shins and arms plus a leather vest that covered him to his throat. His bronze helmet was intricately decorated with lion motifs and had cheek pieces that met at his chin.

He carried two swords, one long and one short, both of bronze. The blades were etched with amazing artistry, the hilts carved. Pamaarans did nothing without decoration.

The chill of the morning and the worry over what was about to happen couldn't quite dampen the heat Lea felt of the remembered night. Deon had taken Thane several more times until Thane had wrestled Deon to the floor and entered *him*.

Then both men had made love to Lea, one after the other, Thane gentle, Deon rough, trading off until she'd fallen into dark slumber. She hadn't wakened until Deon shook her, and she'd opened her eyes to see the sky gray with dawn.

She'd never in her life wanted to get out of bed less than she had that morning.

Felin faced Thane across a circle drawn in the dirt one the seconds had measured and redrawn about a dozen times. Felin also carried two swords and wore leather armor similar to Thane's, his tooled with falcon symbols. Her bloodstone hung around his neck.

Lea half expected Felin to taunt Thane or show off his sword moves, but he waited in silence, like a man ready to get on with things.

Lea and Deon and Justin stood somewhat back from the ring, not allowed to go too near, in case they tried to help Thane. A line of guards, falcon-sword and lion-star, stood between them and the combatants.

Deon couldn't be a second, he'd explained, his arms folded and his jaw tight, because he was too close to the king. The seconds for the Challenge had to be neutral, chosen from the two clans who were not fighting for mastery.

The seconds from the tiger-vessel and dragon-wand clans were as formidable as Thane and Deon. The tiger-vessel guard had tiger tattoos down arms and legs while the dragon-wand guard had a dragon tattoo across his upper back. Tiger-vessel seconded Felin, while dragon-wand seconded Thane.

People from all the clans had streamed in the night before, camping around the perimeter of the plain, as close as they were allowed to come. Now they settled in, quieting to watch the fight to see who ruled their planet.

It took forever to start the actual Challenge. Seers had to bless the place and then the two fighters and the seconds had to confer again to make sure everything had been laid out and done according to the rules.

"I wish they'd get on with it," Lea muttered. "Get it over with and put us out of our misery."

Deon, his hand fidgeting near his sword, nodded grimly. "They take their bloody time. Thane is naturally patient and calm, so it's all right for *him*, but I'd have killed someone by now."

"I'm thinking I would have too. I wish Felin would at least *talk* to him."

"Too late."

Lea turned her attention back to the fighters and saw that at long last, they were starting.

Felin stepped into the ring at the same time Thane squared his shoulders and walked out to meet him. The fond lover of the night before had vanished and a fighting man had taken his place—a man fighting for his people.

The seconds called the start.

Thane and Felin circled each other, each studying the way the other moved and balanced. If this had been a test match between scouts on the Rock, the spectators would have begun jeering, but Thane and Felin weren't here to entertain. This was real.

From what Deon had explained, they'd fight for fifteen Pamaaran minutes, then break for a rest. They'd do this twenty times or until one of them was killed. If they were both alive at the end, then the seconds would declare the winner. The loser would either have to accept the winner's penalty (traditionally, death), or he could kill himself to avoid humiliation.

Some consolation.

"I can't stand to watch," Lea whispered. "But I can't stand to look away, either."

"I know what you mean," Justin murmured beside her.

The spectators were silent. This was no ordinary fight— this would determine the fate of the world and any shout or noise could give advantage to the other side. The morning warmed, the breeze cool, the air dry and blue sky arched overhead. A perfect day, except Thane might die in it.

The first fifteen minutes went by without Thane or Felin getting in a blow. They were still assessing, still evaluating one another when the seconds called time.

Thane moved to a shaded awning where he could drink water and readjust his armor, and where a healer would bind wounds when the combat heated up. Lea and Deon were not allowed to go to him there, either.

"This is maddening." Lea watched Thane the best she could around the wall of guards. He seemed fine, wiping his face with a cloth and downing a cup of water a servant handed him.

In the second fifteen minutes, Felin struck the first blow. Thane easily parried it, but the clang of sword on sword was heartwrenching.

They thrust and parried at each other after that, both of them holding back, saving stamina for the long day ahead. Thane drew first blood in the third go-round, nicking Felin's shoulder. Felin twisted and managed a scratch across Thane's forearm before Thane turned the blade aside. The seconds called time.

Deon watched Thane narrowly as Thane drank water while the servant washed the cut.

"He's not going to make it," he said in a soft voice. "He's already tired."

Lea peered worriedly at the falcon-decorated awning. "Felin doesn't seem any better."

"Maybe not, but do you want to stand here while they chop each other into little bits?"

"What else can we do?" Justin asked from Lea's other side.

Deon glanced around as Thane and Felin entered the ring again. He motioned Lea and Justin to follow him and led the way back toward Thane's circle of tents.

Lea looked back. Thane obviously saw them leaving, but since he wasn't allowed to communicate with them, he could say nothing. She saw his lips compress in a grim line as he swung his sword to meet Felin's.

"Well?" Justin asked when Deon stopped, out of earshot of the guards.

"We can go shield that thing," Deon said. "If it works like Lea said, it might restore the Warding and restore Thane. Then he will kick Felin's ass in the Challenge and we can all get back to normal."

Chapter Fourteen
Choices

ℬ

"I'm not sure what will happen," Lea whispered to him. "Once the shields are in place, the radiation will stop, but who knows if the damage can be repaired?"

"We can try," Deon said impatiently. "It's better than standing here doing nothing."

"He's got a point," Justin put in. Lea could only nod glumly.

As though it had been settled, Deon began striding for the drake pens. Cutie flapped to meet him, showing his teeth in what Lea had come to learn was a greeting.

The drake grooms didn't say a word when Deon saddled Cutie himself and boosted Lea and Justin aboard. They probably thought Deon couldn't stand to stay and watch his lover be killed — the looks they gave Deon were sympathetic.

Lea barely jumped when the drake launched himself into his near-vertical takeoff, though she did hang on tightly to Deon. They flew to the palace first so Deon could collect what Lea needed, then winged to the valley where Lea's burned-out ship waited.

The three guards who had been placed with drakes to watch the wreckage greeted Deon without question. They smiled and waved to him, happy someone had come to relieve their boredom.

Deon let Justin and Lea stun them with the two weapons Deon had retrieved from the palace. Lea had explained to Justin that they had to turn up the stun settings to have effect on the strong Pamaarans. They didn't go down easy, but at last they did.

"I'll make this up to you," Deon told the last one as he collapsed.

Justin surveyed the crumpled hull of Lea's ship in awe as Lea checked the stunned men to make sure they'd be all right. "Shit, Lea, you survived a bad one."

"Tell me about it. I wouldn't have lived at all if not for Deon and Thane."

Justin looked at her with new respect. Then he took out his laser welder Deon had retrieved and began slicing up the hull that was still intact.

"You know what close exposure to that much radiation will do, don't you?" he asked as he worked.

"I have a good idea, yes," Lea said.

"It will kill us, you mean?" Deon asked.

"It might," Lea answered. "It will be bad, anyway."

"I thought as much. But if it restores Thane, it's worth it."

"You can leave, you know, Justin," Lea said. "This isn't your planet, not your fight. You can blast your way out of here—as long as you leave me your laser-welder. Mine is toast from the crash."

"What about you?" Justin asked. "We can teach Deon how to build the shield, then you and I can blast out together."

Lea shook her head. "He'll need help."

Justin punctuated his words by jabbing the welder at the metal plates. "But you'd be stuck here. If killing the radiation seals up the planet's shield, I won't be able to come back for you."

"I know," she answered quietly. "But it will take too long if Deon works alone. He won't be able to stand that much radiation for that amount of time. If we work in shifts, we minimize our exposure."

"I'll leave him my anti-radiation dose. You don't need to stay."

"But he might run out of time. The Challenge will only take another four or so hours and Thane is already wearing out. Plus there's the danger that some of Felin's people might spot Deon before he can finish. Not everyone is at the Challenge."

Deon listened, brows lowering. "If he wants to take you to safety, Lea, I want you to go."

Lea faced him. "I'm not leaving you to do this yourself."

"And I don't want to watch you die." His voice turned savage. "It's already bad enough for me losing Thane. I'd want to know that you were home and happy. So would he."

Lea put her hands on his forearms, loving the feel of his workman's skin and the hard muscle beneath. "But if I go, I'll never see you again."

"I know."

Here then was her choice. Leave Pamaar and the two men she'd fallen in love with or stay here, trapped forever by the Warding.

If she left with Justin, she'd not even be able to find out what happened to Thane and Deon—whether Thane lived and triumphed over Felin or lost to him and died.

Her heart burned, the anguish of the choice churning inside her. If she stayed, she might die trying to restore the shield and even if she lived through *that*, the restored shield would prevent her from ever seeing her home and planet again.

Plus there was no way she could swoop in and rescue Thane from the Challenge, taking him and Deon with her to the Rock, mostly because the four of them would never fit in Justin's ship. Communicating with the Rock to send a bigger ship risked alerting the empire to Pamaar's existence.

Also, she had the feeling Thane would never leave given the chance. He was tied to this place, a part of it, whether he

187

lived or died. He'd be miserable anywhere else, not able to be the man he needed to be. Would she be selfish enough to drag him away to stay with her just so she'd not miss him?

If Thane stayed, Deon stayed. She saw how naïve and silly was her earlier worry that she might drive a wedge between them. An imperial harvesting ship couldn't drive a wedge between them.

She met Deon's eyes and saw the turmoil of indecision warring there as well. He didn't want to let her go, but he also didn't want to risk her life.

"Let me stay," she said. "If I live through this, I won't want to be without you."

"I want you safe," Deon began.

"Screw that. I need to be with Thane." She slanted him a smile. "You understand why."

"Damn you," he growled. "You know, if we make it back, he'll kill me for risking your life."

"I know."

Justin snorted, his laser cutter singing against the metal. "None of us will make it if we don't get a move on."

"You can go," Lea said quickly.

"I'm staying," Justin declared. "No way am I going back to the Rock and telling them I left you alone to face a highly irradiated probe and a pissed off clan leader with a heavy-duty sword. I'd never live it down."

She tried to argue. "But we don't know how much of a window there will be to get your ship out once the probe is shielded."

"I know." He stood up, wiping his face and looking around at the rolling hills, the soft air of the valley. "This place isn't so bad. The empire isn't here and Panece seems nice."

Lea laughed at him and patted his shoulder. "You're the best, Justin. I'm sure Panece will find some way to thank you for helping."

"Sure, if I don't glow in the dark." He leaned down and pulled the last of the plates from the hull. "Let's get this stuff loaded and gone."

* * * * *

Cutie carried the extra weight of the hull plating without noticing it. He flew readily into Felin's territory under Deon's guidance and Lea's directions and landed inside the bowl-shaped valley where Lea had found the probe.

They unloaded the plates then Lea told Deon to send Cutie away. No need to risk him as well.

The drake didn't want to leave Deon, but Deon yelled at him to go find something to eat. Finally Cutie rose into the sky, but he only drifted as far as the wooded hilltop.

Justin hefted a plate. "I can't believe I'm walking into a high radiation situation without three layers of protective gear."

"At least you still have your flight suit."

Justin hadn't relinquished it, though he'd conceded to wear colorful, embroidered Pamaaran robes to hide it at the Challenge. He'd stripped off the robes when they landed to remove the plates from Lea's ship's hull and she found that the skin-fitting black suit looked odd to her. She'd gotten used to the flowing and colorful fabrics of the people of Pamaar.

"It will help some," Justin answered. "We should take turns wearing it if we're taking turns welding. For as much protection as we can get."

Deon eyed his slim build. "I'll never fit into that."

"Yes you will," Lea said. "The cloth has nano-technology in it and will expand or contract to fit your body. Truly one-size-fits-all."

"More words I don't understand."

"You'll believe it when you see it."

189

Justin insisted on going first, with Deon following to learn how to laser weld the plates together over the probe. They had to dig the pieces out of the ground so they could shield all sides and they also had to make sure the plates had no seams.

Lea watched, timing them with the chronometer from Justin's ship. When fifteen minutes had passed, she called them back. "My turn."

Deon watched with interest as she stripped off her clothes to don Justin's suit. "You have the cutest ass, you know that?"

Justin stretched out on the ground, claiming he was saving his strength, but she knew the radiation was already getting to him.

Lea worked until Justin called her back, too soon. They wouldn't have enough time to finish, she worried. She relinquished the suit to Deon, who marveled as it expanded to fit his bulk.

He looked luscious and sexy in the skintight shining black as he marched back to the probe while she and Justin waited in their loose robes.

On one of Lea's stints, she noticed something.

"There won't be enough plates," she panted when she returned to the others. She threw down the laser welder, stripped off the suit and collapsed to the ground. She was weak and sick and knew they couldn't do this much longer.

"Damn," Justin said.

Deon turned a sharp look on him. "I know where we can get more."

Lea sat up in alarm. "No, Deon. He wouldn't be able to leave—ever."

"He said only a couple hours ago he wanted to stay." He fixed his gaze on Justin again. "Did he mean it?"

Justin climbed to his feet. "Yes I meant it." He sighed. "Summon your dragon and let's go harvest my ship."

Lea winced. "Don't say *harvest*."

"Sorry."

"He's not a dragon," Deon said after he whistled for Cutie. "This climate is too hot for dragons—they live in the far north. Drakes are their smaller, dumber cousins."

Cutie landed next to Deon and tried to bite him. Deon snarled and Cutie screeched back.

Even in her growing exhaustion, Lea had to chuckle.

* * * * *

Thane entered the fifteenth phase weary and bloody. He and Felin both had scored many hits, each parrying the other to turn killing blows into recoverable wounds. Thane's thigh burned where Felin's sword had pierced it and Felin was limping from a thrust Thane had landed in the man's back.

Thane's breathing became labored quickly in this round and so did Felin's. The crowd was silent, knowing the end was near. Thane heard only the shuffle of his feet and Felin's on gravel, their grunts as swords swung, the clang of metal hitting metal, the occasional thump of a blade on leather.

Dimly he became aware of a stirring in the guards. He'd seen a drake land but didn't dare turn his head to see which drake.

What Deon had been playing at, grabbing Lea and flying off in the middle of the Challenge, he didn't know. Did he fly her to Justin's ship and tell the young man to take her the hell out of here?

He hoped so, though his heart wrenched at the thought of losing her. But if Felin prevailed, who knew what he'd do to Lea? Better to get her to safety while there was opportunity.

The seconds called time and Thane and Felin retreated. As Thane limped to his pavilion, he saw them—Deon, Lea, Justin—staggering back to their places behind the guards.

So Deon hadn't gotten Lea out of there. Thane's anger surged, then he stopped. The three of them, all grinning like idiots, made it to the edge of the tents and then collapsed and didn't move.

"Damn it." Thane threw down his swords with a clatter and rushed from the pavilion. The startled servant called to him, but Thane shoved his way through guards who tried to stop him. His own guards.

The dragon-wand second panted next to him. "You cannot interfere with the Challenge."

"I'm not interfering," Thane snapped. "I'm within my ten minutes."

"You're not allowed to talk to them."

Thane reached Lea and dropped to one knee beside her, lifting her head into his lap. "I can't talk to them when they're unconscious, can I?"

Lea's face was bright red, as though sunburned, and her skin was dry to the touch. So were Deon's and Justin's, their burn wounds very like Cerena's and Reana's.

"No." Thane lifted Lea and held her close. "Deon, damn you, what the fuck did you do?"

Lea's eyelids fluttered. She stared up at him, her beautiful green eyes blurred and swimming with blood. "We did it. The probe is shielded."

He felt a touch on his leg—Deon's thick hand, his friend and lover smiling up at him. "It's done. Restore the Warding. Be king."

"Why did you take her out there?" Thane demanded, hot tears on his cheeks. "Why didn't you wait?"

"You are dying," Deon rasped. "This was the best way. Justin dosed us with his elixir, but there wasn't enough. We had to share it."

"You shouldn't have gone at all."

A shadow covered Deon and Thane looked up to see Felin standing over them, his swords held ready.

"What the hell is this?" Felin asked quietly, dark eyes furious.

Thane's healing sight saw in him the same fatigue he felt and something more—a trace of the sickness that was killing his people.

"They saved Pamaar," Thane said in a hard voice. "They're dying because you wouldn't listen to me."

"I issued the Challenge. That was enough."

"There was death in your territory, something poisoning the Warding, poisoning Pamaar. They risked their lives to stop it while you were busy swinging your sword."

Felin sneered at him. "Poison you planted there?"

"Poison from beyond the Warding. That's why your clan is the one most sickened by it, why Cerena took sick trying to help you. Lea knew and understood."

"It's like the seer said," the dragon-wand second said, awe in his voice. "When a star falls, the queen will come and the world will be reborn."

"And you believe that bullshit?" Felin asked Thane.

Deon opened his eyes. "I didn't. But I do now. She cured Reana."

"No one could cure Reana. Not even Pamaar's great king." Felin's voice dripped with scorn.

Thane signaled a guard. "Send for Emilie and Reana."

Felin looked surprised. "You didn't put Emilie to death for betraying her clan?"

"She had good reason to do what she did."

"Yap, yap, yap," Deon growled from the ground. He tried to meet Thane's gaze, but it was obvious he couldn't see. "All I hear is talk. Get your ass to the Warding and restore it, oh my king."

"He hasn't won the Challenge," Felin said.

"So? You're a walking dead man if you don't let him fix the Warding and heal you. You'll end up just like me."

Felin opened his mouth to say more, but closed it and stared at the child running toward him, followed by a watchful Emilie and two guards. Reana hurried in all innocence toward the little group, trusting her mother to follow.

"Lord Thane," she called happily. She stopped in a swirl of silk as she caught sight of Lea in his arms. "What happened to Lady Lea? Is she all right?"

Reana knelt and touched Lea's cheek while Felin looked over the little girl in astonishment. "You healed her?"

"Almost. Forfeit the Challenge, Felin, or neither of us will be standing in the end. Let me re-bind with the Warding. If I fail, I'll die and you can try. If I live, I heal your people."

"Forfeit?" Felin snapped. "When I'm winning? I am the only one who can restore the Warding now."

Lea opened her eyes. They were filled with red, the green faded, and like Deon, she could no longer see. "Don't be stupider than you really are, Felin," she whispered. "Your clan needs you. Don't let what we did be wasted."

Thane watched Felin's angry words die on his lips. Felin didn't trust Thane and he wanted to win, that was clear. But Felin was also a clan leader first and foremost. The welfare of the falcon-sword clan was his responsibility, one he took very seriously.

The tattoos on his face smoothed and he lowered his swords.

"Do the binding," he said in a resigned voice. "But if your powers aren't restored, I kill you."

"Done," Thane said.

"About bloody time," Deon grated, then his eyes closed and his body went limp.

Chapter Fifteen
Rebirth

ॐ

Thane glowed. Lea pried open her eyes to see Thane standing on the edge of the precipice over the Warding cave, his arms outstretched. The Warding below responded to him, sending bright red and blue and magenta light over Thane and the entire cave.

Thane's naked body glowed in response. He seemed to stretch toward the crystal ceiling, growing taller and stronger, infused with power.

He was a beautiful man, the light outlining every muscle and sinew. He was erect, his cock a long, gleaming length, as though the Warding's touch filled him with sexual excitement.

He walked in a strong, measured stride, not to Lea lying on the rocky ground of the cave between Deon and Justin, but to Felin who waited with his guards, the clan leader still in his leather armor. Thane stretched out his glowing hands and placed them on Felin's head.

Because Deon, Lea and Justin were so close to death, the leaders of the four clans had agreed that Thane could have them brought with him when he renewed the binding instead of approaching the Warding alone. Felin had agreed only if Thane proved himself by curing Felin first. *Figures,* Lea thought.

Felin's body jerked. A guard at his side moved, but Felin stopped him. "No. It's glorious. Oh gods."

He threw his head back, his brown-and-golden hair falling around him, his eyes closed in ecstasy. He reached for Thane as though he would embrace him then dropped his arms, just in time remembering they were rivals, not lovers.

Felin shuddered again, then he stepped back from Thane, breaking the touch.

"By the gods," he said hoarsely.

"I'm glad you feel better," Thane said in his tone of quiet humor. "I'll take care of my loved ones now."

Loved ones. Lea liked the sound of that. The next thing she knew Thane cradled her against his strong, bare chest, his skin still glowing.

"Heal Deon first," she gasped. "He was exposed longer…he kept going when we couldn't."

"Screw you," Deon said, his eyes closed and his voice so weak it was barely audible. "Heal her quick, Thane, so she'll shut up."

Thane smiled as he cuddled Lea close. She suddenly felt a burning through her body, followed by a sensation of incredible joy and incredible desire. She wound her arms around Thane's neck and met his lips in a long, needing kiss.

"Thank you," Deon breathed. "Thank all the gods. Now hurry up, lover. Me and Justin, we don't have all day and you're going to love what I have in mind to show my gratitude."

* * * * *

The next days were eventful. Felin declared Thane the winner of the Challenge, his previous animosity subdued. Thane by right could have had Felin killed and Felin's heir declared clan leader, but he'd decided on amnesty.

He knew Felin had been hostile only because he'd been a desperate man trying to save his people, as desperate as Emilie had been. Thane declared Felin pardoned and Felin accepted without rancor.

Before he departed for his own territory, Felin asked to see Lea. Outside Thane's tent, Felin lifted the bloodstone from around his neck and held it out to her while Deon stood, tense, behind her.

"I think this is yours," Felin said. "Queen of Pamaar."

Thane waited, not daring to breathe, to see what Lea would do. Felin was acknowledging her and the prophecy and, believe it or not, apologizing.

Lea took the bloodstone in her hands and gazed at it for a few moments, then she dropped it back into Felin's palm and closed his hand around it. "You keep it. It's my gift."

Felin stared at her, mystified. "You're giving me a gift? I thought you'd want to shove it up my ass."

Lea smiled. "Think of it as a pledge between my clan and yours, a symbol of friendship and trust. Besides, it's a perfectly good bloodstone. Why waste it on your ass?"

"Touché, my queen."

"The falcon tattoo — *that* I'd love to shove up your ass."

Felin only smiled and shot Thane a self-satisfied look. Thane smiled right back, because Thane's idea for the tattoos Lea would receive had been inspired by the falcon.

Felin finally departed and Thane took his people home.

He spent much of his time after that healing the sick and re-infusing other healers with his power, sending them into falcon-sword territory first. The Warding was whole and strong, no dead places anywhere, and Thane felt the power of Pamaar restored with it.

He wasn't sure how it had happened — Lea's babbled explanation that the Warding was part organic and had psychically repaired itself once the radiation stopped bleeding into it made no sense to him.

She and Justin had showed him numbers and colors on their instruments, talking excitedly together, and Thane had only smiled and let them run on. He'd felt the Warding embrace him again, he and its power keeping the planet safe, and he was satisfied with that.

The Warding repaired meant that Justin could not take off in his ship. He seemed somewhat glum about being stuck on Pamaar, but not too much so. Lea explained that Justin, like herself, had no family on the Rock and friends only in the scout corps.

Justin had brightened when Deon asked him to form a small scouting corps in his guards and to train them to keep an eye out for anything else that might come from beyond the Warding. If they'd had regular patrols years ago, Deon growled, they might have discovered the presence of the probe at once and destroyed it.

Emilie, likewise, was released after her trial, much to Lea's delight. The trial's verdict was that she'd done wrong and would face consequences, but that she'd acted out of the understandable instinct to save her daughter. She had to forfeit the privilege of being a royal courtesan, but she seemed happy to have more time to devote to Reana.

And Deon—was Deon.

Deon's initial healing had been loud, with Deon shouting his climax through the caves until guards had come running to see what was the matter.

They'd found Deon lying on his back, naked, with a smile on his face, saying, "That was the best—*ever*."

He'd wanted another healing in private in the tent, with Lea nearby. As soon as Thane had laid his hands on Deon and sent healing power through him, Deon had grabbed Thane and rolled him down to the cushions. They'd had rather ferocious sex after that, Deon in Lea, Thane in Deon, then Lea pleasuring them both at the same time.

In the darkness after all that ecstasy, Thane lay exhausted. And yet energy burned through his tiredness, strength restored by the Warding. A gift from Lea and his lover, Deon.

"The only bad thing," Deon mumbled sleepily, his head on Thane's shoulder, "is that you're king again. No more me beautifully fucking you."

Thane let his hand drift through Deon's long hair. "I'm going to work to get that law changed."

"Good idea, but it will take forever. You know the council." His eyes twinkled. "I was great, though, wasn't I?"

"The best."

Lea rolled to her knees beside them, awake again. "Oh please. I'll be the judge of who is best."

Deon sat up, his grin widening, the man at his full strength. "Will you? This could be interesting."

It was. They made love to her all night, first Thane, then Deon, until Lea slid into sleep. Deon gave her a mock-outraged stare when she tiredly declared the contest a draw.

After the first heady days of rejoicing came the announcement that the king would marry Lea, the lady who'd come from a falling star. More celebrations, the hardworking Pamaarans of all clans dropping daily tasks to join in the festivities.

A royal wedding took much planning, enough to drive Thane mad, but he went along with it, knowing his people would love the pageantry. Deon escaped with his drakes and his new scout corps, but Lea remained, patiently learning Pamaaran etiquette.

"You two plan the wedding," Deon would growl. "I'll plan the wedding *night.*"

But one ceremony Deon remained for was Lea's tattoos.

Soft lights glowed in Thane's bedchamber, two silk-clad musicians plucked instruments in the corner and the tattoo artist knelt on the cushioned bed, ready to work.

Lea blushed when Thane helped her disrobe, but the artist only sorted his needles and inks, oblivious to her beautiful female flesh. To him she was a canvas for his art, nothing more.

Thane stretched out next to her, his body uncovered except for his loincloth. He'd pulled his hair back, braids, beads and all to reveal his tattoos, the lion across his back, the pentacles on his arms and chest, the interlocked lion designs on his thighs.

Deon, also in only a loincloth, lounged at the foot of the bed. The artist ran a pleased gaze over the lions on Deon's arms and pelvis, his own work.

He held up his instruments, ready to remove the falcon tattoo, but Thane stopped him.

"I want her to keep it," he said.

Lea had been biting her lip but now looked at Thane in surprise. "You do? Why?"

"I want it to be known that my queen will look out for all clans, not just the lion-star. She will be a great healer and walk among them all when they need her." He looked into Lea's stunned green eyes and smiled. "I want her to have a dragon and a tiger as well as lions."

The artist stared, openmouthed. "Such a thing has never been done before, my lord."

"A queen has never healed the entire planet before," Thane said. "But Lea has already done so. She will be of every clan. We will start a new tradition."

Deon laughed from the end of the bed. "You're crazy. I've always said so."

Lea's eyes softened. "No, he isn't."

Thane's blood warmed, even though Deon still shook his head. The artist shrugged as though to say, *You're the king*, then he went to work.

* * * * *

"I like this one best." Two days later, Deon ran his fingers down Lea's back where a lion reached down her spine, its clawed foot resting on the small of her back.

She tingled with pleasure at his touch. Thane and the artist had indeed made the tattooing painless and Thane had healed her skin quickly. He'd still made her rest before doing anything strenuous—most Pamaarans didn't get so many tattoos in one sitting, he said, but acquired them over a lifetime.

Tonight Thane and Deon had brought her into Thane's bedroom to admire her. She lay naked on her stomach while they touched her body and traced the artist's strokes.

A dragon coiled on the back of her right leg and a tiger crouched on the back of her left. The falcon still spread across her hip and the tattoo artist had interlaced the designs so they made a pleasing whole.

Thane gently rolled her over. A chain of pentacles laced across her collarbone, two tiny lions danced above her nipples and another lion twined around her naval. She'd not let them tattoo her face, but she'd allowed a lion down her throat that blended into the pentacles across her chest.

All had been done in an astonishing array of colors. Most tattoos she'd seen before this—and she'd not seen many—had been black or dark blue.

Hers were a rainbow of gold (for the lions), scarlet, blue, green, silver, violet, black and brown. The dragon was brilliant green and red, the tiger orange and black and the pentacles many and varied hues.

Deon licked the lion on her belly and ended up with his tongue in her navel. She laughed and squirmed.

"You know," he said to Thane, warming her skin with his lips. "I thought we'd wait for the wedding night, but this might be a better time. To celebrate her becoming a true lion-star."

Thane's dark eyes sparked with interest. "Ah, that plan. Impatient, are you?"

"Damn right I am."

Lea glanced at Thane in suspicion. "What plan? I haven't heard of any plan."

Deon grinned. "The two of us—in you. Showing that we three are finally one."

Lea's heart began to pound. "I still don't know if I'm ready for that."

"You didn't think you were ready for tattoos," Deon pointed out.

"True."

"It is up to you, love." Thane brushed his fingertips across her chain of pentacles. "Will you bind with us?"

She studied them both, Thane with his white-blond hair such a contrast to his dark eyes, eyes that held wisdom and power and gentleness. Deon with his swarthy skin and warrior's sinewy arms, black hair and wicked eyes. Thane to love her in great tenderness—Deon to make it wild.

"I have a feeling I'll regret this in the morning," she said shakily. "But all right."

Deon kissed her bellybutton. "We'll wake you up nice and sweet tomorrow. You won't regret a thing."

"We'd never hurt you," Thane said, his voice warm. "We want your pleasure, love."

"And to enjoy every minute of pleasing you," Deon put in.

Lea touched Thane's face, and Deon's. "I'm so in love with you. Both of you."

Thane's throat moved, as though he held back emotion. Deon's eyes flared and his smile broadened. "Good. This will be even better."

* * * * *

They did it by having Thane enter her first. He spread himself beneath her and she slid onto him, closing her eyes as she felt his thick hardness reaching inside her. He was so big and felt so incredible.

She lay down on him as Deon instructed and felt the cool bite of lube on her anal star. Then Deon's weight on her, then his slick stem easing its way into her.

Lea stifled a groan. Deon had made love to her plenty by now and she was used to his wide cock inside her, but nothing prepared her for this.

"Shh." Thane's hands roved her body, his healing spreading through her. The electric feel of it excited her and relaxed her at the same time, allowing her to open to Deon.

He went slowly, slowly, while Thane soothed her and then he was all the way in.

The two men she loved, their cocks in her at the same time. She could feel both of them stretching her, pulling her, could feel them touching each other through her walls.

She started to scream. She couldn't stand it and yet she wanted it to go on and on.

"I can't," she cried.

Thane touched Deon's arm. "Ease back."

"No!" Lea looked back at Deon. His eyes were heavy, his face flushed. "No, please stay in me. Make me take it."

Deon smiled. "All right." He slid in even farther. "Gods, I love you."

Thane laced his hand through Deon's hair and pulled him down for a kiss. Lea turned her head so she could join in and the three of them let lips and tongues tangle the best they could.

"I love you, Lea," Deon whispered, nipping her ear. "Love you so much."

Thane remained silent, but he traced Lea's lips with the tip of his tongue. She felt her climax build and overflow—too soon, but goddess, it was *good.*

She writhed between them, all thoughts fleeing. She felt only tingling darkness and their two cocks inside her, heard only her own screams of joy. Then Thane's seed scalded her, followed by Deon's, filling her.

A black wave of sleep rushed at her and when she swam out of it, she was lying on her side facing Thane. Deon snored behind her, but Thane watched her with his midnight-dark eyes.

"Are you all right?" he asked in a low voice.

Lea started to answer with a neutral *yes*, then remembered the incredible sensation of them both inside her and shivered.

"Goddess, that was…" She drew in a long breath. "The most incredible…" She brushed her hand over her face, words failing her.

Thane's low laugh shook the bed. "I will take that as *good.*"

"Very, very good."

He lost his smile. "I know that you are truly stranded here now. I've made you lion-star, and of Pamaar, but I can't help feeling that maybe this is not what you wish."

His gaze flicked away from her, as though he didn't want to watch her reaction to his words.

Lea cupped his face in her hands and brought his focus back to her. "I made my choice. Out in the valley when we went to shield the probe, I knew Justin and I could fly out of there and leave you and Deon to whatever fate waited for you. That's when I chose."

"Why didn't you go?"

"Because I needed to stay. Back on the Rock, they need scouts, but there are dozens graduating from flight school every month. They'll fill my place with another, maybe someone with better skills than me—Justin too. But there's only one of you." She stroked the pads of her thumbs across his cheekbones. "I wasn't about to let you die when I could possibly save you."

"You couldn't have known you'd be successful."

"I was willing to take the chance. So was Deon. We had a better chance if we worked together, even Justin saw that."

"If it hadn't worked, I would have watched you die," he said, voice hard.

"It was worth it. If Deon had worked alone, he definitely would have died. I wasn't letting that happen."

Thane suddenly scooped her to him and held her in a savage grip. "Don't you ever do that again," he said against her hair. "Never sacrifice yourself for me. Do you understand me?"

Lea loosened his hold and saw tears standing in his eyes. "I can't promise that. I love you, I'm going to marry you and be your queen. Heck, I even let you have me tattooed and *that* was truly scary."

"I can't lose you. I can't. I need you." He brushed her hair back from her face. "I love you."

"I love you too." She kissed the tip of his nose. "That's the whole point."

He kissed her then, long and loving, while her heart ached with joy.

When they eased apart, she laughed a little. "As weird as it is, I love Deon too. I want you to love each other and I want you to love me. It's like love doubled."

Thane laughed, a true laugh, ringing to the ceiling. "With Deon's enthusiasm, more like love tripled."

His laughter woke Deon, who grunted, his snoring ceasing. He scrubbed his hand over his face, then loomed over Lea like Cutie rising over the drake pens.

"So much talking," he growled. "If you're not sleeping, why aren't we fucking?"

Lea laughed as she readily rolled over on the bed for Deon. As Deon started kissing her, her hand remained twined in Thane's, and she smiled into his warm eyes.

Also by Allyson James

ଞ

Christmas Cowboy

Double Trouble

Ellora's Cavemen: Dreams of the Oasis I (*anthology*)

Ellora's Cavemen: Jewels of the Nile IV (*anthology*)

Ellora's Cavemen: Seasons of Seduction I (*anthology*)

Howlin'

Tales of the Shareem: Aiden and Ky

Tales of the Shareem: Maia and Rylan

Tales of the Shareem: Rees

Tales of the Shareem: Rio

About the Author

ஐ

Allyson James began writing at age eight. She wrote love stories before she knew what romances were, dreaming of the day when her books would appear at libraries and bookstores. One day, she, decided to stop dreaming and do it for real.

After a long struggle and inevitable rejections, she at last sold a romance novel, then to her surprise several mystery novels, more romances, and erotic romances to Ellora's Cave, and became a bestselling author. She writes under several pseudonyms, has been nominated for and won Romantic Times Reviewer's Choice awards, and has had starred reviews in Booklist and Top Pick reviews in Romantic Times.

Allyson loves to write, read, hike, and build dollhouses. She met her soul mate when she was eighteen, traveled around the world with him, and settled down with him in the desert southwest.

Allyson welcomes comments from readers. You can find her website and email address on her author bio page at www.ellorascave.com.

Tell Us What You Think

We appreciate hearing reader opinions about our books. You can email us at Comments@EllorasCave.com.

Why an electronic book?

We live in the Information Age — an exciting time in the history of human civilization, in which technology rules supreme and continues to progress in leaps and bounds every minute of every day. For a multitude of reasons, more and more avid literary fans are opting to purchase e-books instead of paper books. The question from those not yet initiated into the world of electronic reading is simply: *Why?*

1. *Price.* An electronic title at Ellora's Cave Publishing and Cerridwen Press runs anywhere from 40% to 75% less than the cover price of the exact same title in paperback format. Why? Basic mathematics and cost. It is less expensive to publish an e-book (no paper and printing, no warehousing and shipping) than it is to publish a paperback, so the savings are passed along to the consumer.

2. *Space.* Running out of room in your house for your books? That is one worry you will never have with electronic books. For a low one-time cost, you can purchase a handheld device specifically designed for e-reading. Many e-readers have large, convenient screens for viewing. Better yet, hundreds of titles can be stored within your new library — on a single microchip. There are a variety of e-readers from different manufacturers. You can also read e-books on your PC or laptop computer. (Please note that Ellora's Cave does not endorse any specific brands.

You can check our websites at www.ellorascave.com or www.cerridwenpress.com for information we make available to new consumers.)

3. *Mobility.* Because your new e-library consists of only a microchip within a small, easily transportable e-reader, your entire cache of books can be taken with you wherever you go.

4. *Personal Viewing Preferences.* Are the words you are currently reading too small? Too large? Too... ANNOYING? Paperback books cannot be modified according to personal preferences, but e-books can.

5. *Instant Gratification.* Is it the middle of the night and all the bookstores near you are closed? Are you tired of waiting days, sometimes weeks, for bookstores to ship the novels you bought? Ellora's Cave Publishing sells instantaneous downloads twenty-four hours a day, seven days a week, every day of the year. Our webstore is never closed. Our e-book delivery system is 100% automated, meaning your order is filled as soon as you pay for it.

Those are a few of the top reasons why electronic books are replacing paperbacks for many avid readers.

As always, Ellora's Cave and Cerridwen Press welcome your questions and comments. We invite you to email us at Comments@ellorascave.com or write to us directly at Ellora's Cave Publishing Inc., 1056 Home Avenue, Akron, OH 44310-3502.

COMING TO A BOOKSTORE NEAR YOU!

ELLORA'S CAVE

Bestselling Authors Tour

UPDATES AVAILABLE AT

WWW.ELLORASCAVE.COM

erridwen, the Celtic Goddess of wisdom, was the muse who brought inspiration to storytellers and those in the creative arts. Cerridwen Press encompasses the best and most innovative stories in all genres of today's fiction. Visit our site and discover the newest titles by talented authors who still get inspired - much like the ancient storytellers did, once upon a time.

Cerridwen Press

www.cerridwenpress.com

Discover for yourself why readers can't get enough
of the multiple award-winning publisher
Ellora's Cave.

Whether you prefer e-books or paperbacks,
be sure to visit EC on the web at
www.ellorascave.com
for an erotic reading experience that will leave you
breathless.

Lightning Source UK Ltd.
Milton Keynes UK
24 November 2009

146660UK00001B/84/P